English and the Indian Short Story

Essays in Criticism

English and the Indian Short Story
Essays in Criticism

Edited by
Mohan Ramanan
P. Sailaja

Orient Longman

ORIENT LONGMAN LIMITED

Registered Office
3-6-272 Himayatnagar, Hyderabad 500 029 (A.P.), INDIA

Other Offices
Bangalore, Bhopal, Bhubaneshwar, Calcutta, Chandigarh, Chennai, Ernakulam, Guwahati, Hyderabad, Jaipur, Lucknow, Mumbai, New Delhi, Patna

First published 2000

ISBN 81 250 1660 0

Typeset by
Scribe Consultants
New Delhi 110 029

Printed in India at
Baba Barkha Nath Printers
New Delhi 110 015

Published by
Orient Longman Limited
1/24 Asaf Ali Road
New Delhi 110 002

Acknowledgements

This book is the result of a National Seminar on 'English and the Indian Short Story' held in August 1994 at the Department of English, University of Hyderabad. The Seminar was funded by the University Grants Commission's Special Assistance Programme which the Department enjoys. It is a pleasure to acknowledge the assistance of several people in the organisation of the seminar and the preparation of this book.

Our primary debt is to all the participants in the Seminar who promptly submitted their papers for publication and conscientiously answered our editorial queries.

We express our appreciation of the editorial advice offered to us by S. Viswanathan, Sudhakar Marathe and Alladi Uma at various stages in the preparation of this book.

We thank Prof. Shiv K. Kumar for inaugurating the Seminar and Alok Bhalla for giving a special talk. To the University of Hyderabad administrative and supporting staff, to Prof. K.K. Ranganadhacharyulu, former Dean of Humanities, University of Hyderabad, to Professors Probal Dasgupta, Shashi Mudiraj and R. Srihari and to all our colleagues and students in the Department of English, we express our thanks for their valuable contributions. We also thank G. Rajendra Prasad, M. Satyanarayana Murthy and D. Narsaiah of the Department of English, for secretarial and administrative help.

Contents

Acknowledgements *v*

Introduction 1

My Writing, My Times 10
ASHOKAMITRAN

The Malayalam Short Story—Evolution,
Influences, Original Perspectives 19
VASANTHI SANKARANARAYANAN

The Perennial Popularity of R.K. Narayan:
An Analysis of 'Father's Help' 27
LAKSHMI CHANDRA

When East is West: A Thematic and Stylistic Analysis of
Bharati Mukherjee's *The Middleman And Other Stories* 35
P.A. ABRAHAM

The Immigrant Sensibility in Bharati Mukherjee's
The Middleman And Other Stories 46
K. SANTHANAM

Indian Englishes and the Indian Short Story in English 53
T. SRIRAMAN

Language Dialectic and Fakir Mohan's
Rhetoric of Progress 68
SACHIDANANDA MOHANTY

English in the Telugu Short Story: Some Observations 75
M. KESHAV

Problems in Translating 'Sati Savitri' 81
M. SRIDHAR AND ALLADI UMA

English and the 'Country' Short Story in India: A Responsibility 86
SUDHAKAR MARATHE

Of Other Voices: Mahasweta Devi's Short Stories Translated by Gayatri Chakravorty Spivak 94
TUTUN MUKHERJEE

Male Culture, Female Strategies 106
RANJANA HARISH

Cheated and Exploited: Women in Kamala Das's Short Stories 117
D. MURALI MANOHAR

En-Gendering Narratives: A Reading of 'Black Horse Square' 124
REKHA PAPPU

Student Responses to an Intermediate Text: A Case Study 135
NIRMALA RITA NAIR

The Indian Short Story: Towards a Location Chart 146
S. VISWANATHAN

Contributors 152

Introduction

The short story has emerged as a significant genre in Indo-English literature as well as in other Indian literatures. The impact of English on short-story writing in India, both in Indian English and in Indian languages, has been considerable. Insufficient critical attention has been paid in India to this relationship if not to the genre. In an attempt to address this issue, the Department of English, University of Hyderabad, organised a National Seminar in August 1994 on 'English and the Indian Short Story'. The papers collected in this volume were presented at that seminar.

In India, English language and literature cannot be viewed unproblematically, but must be seen as being deeply implicated in an ideology linked to colonial rule. Many of the papers in this volume explore the impact of this ideology on the emergence of the Indian short story. Several papers are also interested in the way English as a language has shaped short story writing in India. An assumption informing this volume is that the Indo-British literary and cultural encounter shaped modern Indian sensibility.

Participants at the seminar were encouraged to explore this question in concrete ways. The impressive body of writing in English by Indians raises questions as to why English is used, how it is employed and what it does to literature in the regional languages. These are old questions but need to be asked again and answered as specifically as possible. The following papers on writers as diverse as R.K. Narayan, Kamala Das, Bharati Mukherjee, Khushwant Singh and Shashi Tharoor raise these questions, and attempt to answer them.

A lot of the writing in the various Indian languages is fortunately available to us in English translation. Papers at the seminar therefore addressed the problems of translation, the losses and gains of translation, as well as the questions of equivalence, deviation and untranslatability. These questions are dealt with in papers exploring short stories in Telugu, Marathi, Bengali and Oriya.

Many of the Indian writers intersperse their writing in Indian languages with English words, phrases and sentences. This is an interesting dimension to the question of the impact of English on the Indian short story, not to speak of the fact that these writers are actually reflecting social realities. Some papers show how English as a language is used in stories in Indian languages to distinguish characters, for comic effect and for a whole range of fictional purposes.

Many participants focussed consciously on matters of language. For the purposes of this seminar, which encouraged such a focus, language was defined broadly to include grammar, structure and the use (conscious or unconscious) of devices such as imagery, metaphor, tone, setting, etc. These papers thus display a variety of preoccupations, approaches and methods. We have both general and localised surveys of the development of the short story in India, papers focussing on women's writing and feminist concerns, papers on Indo-English short stories, and stories in translation.

II

There has been a marked increase in short story writing in recent decades. These are many reasons for this. The short story can easily reach a wide audience through popular magazines and newspapers. Practically every major newspaper has a short-story section as standard fare. Literary journals like *Indian Literature*, and the *Yatra* series feature short stories on a regular basis. The *Katha* series is specifically devoted to publishing Indian language stories in English translation. Magazines have always been in the forefront in promoting the short story—witness the example of *The Illustrated Weekly of India*. More than any other literary form, the short story is a ready and easily available barometer of human experience; that is reason enough for its popularity. When individuals like Khushwant Singh or Kamala Das or Bharati Mukherjee publish either a complete collection of short stories or a selection, it is another indication of not only the popularity of the form but of the fact that these writers have arrived. Moreover, collections of translated stories by writers in Indian languages like Vaikom Muhammad Basheer or Premchand or Satyajit Ray only enhance the possibilities for students of the Indian short story. These possibilities have to do with the study of repesentations of India in all its specificity and diversity, and a focus on the complexity of form in these stories. The appearance, in recent years of several short story anthologies devoted to women writers, and of Arjun Dangle's edition of Dalit short stories, *Homeless in My Land,* signals the increasing importance of marginalised and minority groups and the fact that literature emanating from these groups will make its presence felt, if it has not already done so.

Short story writing is not new to India. As a literary form, the Indian short story, or to be precise, the 'brief' story in a variety of sub-forms, goes back to the *Kathasaritasagara,* the *Panchatantra,* the *Jataka Tales,* and to the tradition of folk-lore and legend, to the richness of which, a compiler like A.K. Ramanujan has done justice in his recent *Folk Tales from India.* In matters of strategies for story-telling, or weaving a narrative, or creating a *frisson* or generating suspense, Indians have a fine native provenance to go by and need not seek Western models. Without doubt the Indian short story is built on strong indigenous foundations. However, that is not the focus of this volume. Its emphasis is on the relation of English to the Indian short story. From that point of view we need to acknowledge the literary impact of the West and particularly of English on the shaping of the modern Indian sensibility as reflected in short story writing. S. Viswanathan's valedictory address, included in this volume, charts these relationships.

British colonial rule and English proved to be catalysts in the creation of this modern sensibility. This modern Indian sensibility, as we shall see, is deeply influenced by the experience of colonial rule and the sentiment of nationalism. Many short stories, particularly at the turn of the nineteenth century or in the early decades of the twentieth, inevitably turn to the Indo-

British encounter. Munshi Premchand's stories constitute a classic instance of this preoccupation. He was writing at a time when nationalist sentiment was at its height, British rule was repressive, and independence was still years away. Yet, ironically the impact of the West had itself generated nationalist ideas amongst Indians. In a story like 'Namak Ka Daroga' ('The Salt-Inspector'), an important phase of the nationalist struggle culminating at Dandi is symbolically presented in the incident of salt being smuggled. Or, take a story like 'The Resignation' which is about a Babu, apparently a typical file-pushing clerk of the British Raj, who finally rebels against his arrogant, blustering and bullying Sahib.

If the historical fact of British rule enabled short-story writing, the other momentous historical event of the Partition has also produced memorable literary expression. Alok Bhalla's lecture at the seminar (not included here) which was a version of his 'Introduction' to *Stories about the Partition of India*, a three-volume collection of Partition stories, charted this epoch as embodied in English translations of stories from major Indian languages. Partition stories were of different kinds. There were fundamentalist stories espousing the cause of Muslims and Pakistan or of Hindus and India. These gave a particular exclusivist thrust to history, simplifying it and thus distorting it. But more comlex attitudes were also brought to bear on the writing of short stories. There were many which spoke of the horror and violence of Partition, the pity of it all. Yet others, and these were the best and most memorable, invoked the memory of it in an effort to recover balance. Writing of this kind was therapeutic, an antidote to any possible repetition of the violence and of the attitudes evinced in rabid insularity. A good example of this is Manto's 'Toba Tek Singh', a touching and powerful indictment of Partition and the violence of that event, with the principal character, a lunatic, speculating about the fate of his village, and dying in his search for it; others are Vatsyayan's 'Getting Even', and Ibrahim Jaleez's 'Grave Turned Inside Out'.

Historical events have continued to have their impact on the Indian short story. With Independence, the reconstruction of India and the assertion of a national identity brought in some of the early work of Indo-English masters like R.K. Narayan, Raja Rao and Mulk Raj Anand. The cultivation of a landscape, and topography around the semi-fictional Malgudi, as representative of a South Indian small town, complete with railway station, main street, school etc., is R.K. Narayan's special forte. This taken together with the metaphysical speculations of Raja Rao and Mulk Raj Anand's focus on the disadvantaged and dispossesed, gave expression to three aspects of the life of an emerging nation. Narayan presented an idealised picture of a small town and its people. Rao focussed on 'spiritual' India both in his characters and landscape, while Anand provided a delineation of the lower strata of Indian society. Between them, one might say, a large section of India, with the exception perhaps of the metropolis, was covered.

As the decades moved on, other emphases took over. Anita Desai, for example, writes about the psychological problems of the Indian middle class with insight and intensity. Here one perhaps sees a shift from what Sudhakar Marathe in his paper calls 'country' fiction to the city and urban experience with its attendant problems and conflicts and its search for values. Kamala Das is concerned with the condition of women and the way in which they are betrayed by society. So from the political, social and spiritual levels, the short story modulated into the personal, the private and the psychological. New sexual mores, fresh possibilities in human relations, marriage, motherhood are explored. Kamala Das is a prime example of this, but women's writing has expanded the significance of the genre, widened its horizons and made the short story a potent vehicle for social and psychological change. The distinguished critic, B. Rajan, wondered in 1965 whether the Indian tradition with its capacity for assimilation could come to terms with the new without eroding its fundamental character. Rajan's prescience is remarkable but he need not have worried because the contemporary Indian short story has become an effective literary tool for the promotion of a secularised democratic culture quite at odds with the traditional pieties.

We have thus far spoken of the Indian English short story but modernity is just as available in stories in the Indian languages. Writers in these languages have learned from both English and non-English masters—Irish, French, Russian. In sheer complexity and in the exploration of those new experiences Rajan speaks about, perhaps they have been ahead of writers in English.

Politics and history continue to play a vital role in short story production. What Naipaul has called a 'million mutinies' or what Partha Chatterjee calls the 'fragmentation of the nation', have had their impact too. The large number of stories about women as represented in, for instance, Lakshmi Holmstrom's *The Inner Courtyard*, which contains writing both in English and in Indian languages clearly shows the nation in its specificities. The lesson is driven home of course much more clearly by the writers in the various Indian languages. The Indian short story in English is only reflective of one facet, that too, a minor facet of Indian life. India exists to a large extent in her languages and in the specific, in particular locations, societies, geographical spaces. Stories by Basheer, Mahasweta Devi, Ashokamitran and others in the various Indian languages clearly represent the plurality of Indian life and India's diversity.

III

At this point, given the seminal role it has played in this domain, a few reflections on English in India would be appropriate. Let us straightaway assert that English is in India to stay. The Indian short story in English too is an impressively large corpus of work and has much to tell us about how the English language has been abrogated and appropriated for Indian uses. The experiments of R.K. Narayan, Raja Rao and Mulk Raj Anand now look modest, yet when these writers began their careers, they were revolutionary in confronting the colonial legacy in the colonial tongue. It is on the basis of their work that writers down the decades, and latter-day writers like Salman Rushdie or Shashi Tharoor have carried out their experiments with the English language. This was in a sense a second revolution, at a point when English became a facile tool in their hands. These contemporary writers could take some things for granted and could function without having to be too anxious about the burden of English as their seniors were. The tendency of some observers to downplay English and to promote other Indian languages, as though English were not Indian too, fails to give sufficient credit to what the Indian writers in English have achieved. Theirs is no mean achievement, and the essays in this volume by Lakshmi Chandra, Abraham, Santhanam, Murali Manohar, and Sriraman highlight the way in which Indian English writers have fused theme and technique to produce notable work.

However, the importance of the Indian languages cannot be ignored either. One cannot deny the many Indias—real and compelling—represented in the different languages. In technique too these writings down the decades have displayed great sophistication. The old realist tradition of the linear narrative has been deconstructed and fantasy, magic realism, symbolism and collage inform recent writings as much as they do the work of the Indian writers writing in English. Indeed, in stories in the Indian languages these experiments can also be seen as indigenous and having Indian roots, and not necessarily as the result of Western or English influence. That is all to the good, but the important thing is that for a wider dissemination of these native traditions, translations into English are necessary. This point is brought home in the essays of Sudhakar Marathe, Alladi Uma and M. Sridhar, Ranjana Harish, Tutun Mukherjee, Rekha Pappu, Sachidananda Mohanty and Vasanthi Sankaranarayanan. In a flexible and considerably expanded form therefore, English seems poised to function as an important element in the literary and cultural life of the country. To say that the Indian languages have not been influenced by English, or to claim that the site for cultural struggle is to be found *only* in them and *not* in the English stories, is to ignore the complexity of the issue.

An even more relevant question is the one about Standard English. Translations done into Standard English can seriously distort the original idiom. What Marathe calls 'country fiction' or what in general may be called dialectal speech used to capture specific Indian experience, perhaps requires exercises in deviance. At the same time, a balance is needed because if the translation is into English, it is equally important to preserve the genius of that language and to ensure intelligibility. Some interesting insights into what happens when language is used deviantly are available in T. Sriraman's account of Khushwant Singh and Shashi Tharoor. And then again, since we are involved with pedagogy, Nirmala Nair's contribution makes many valuable points about the problems of comprehension of texts prescribed for study. Too much deviance from Standard English, she emphasises, can also pose problems.

Finally, we believe that Khushwant Singh's assertion that Indians continue to write short stories well because they are following the 'rules' is valuable. The short story predictably is short, but how short? It should be possible to read a short story in one sitting. But what is a sitting? There are no mechanical answers to these questions. The Indian short stories of today generally tend to have magnitude—that Aristotelian category which in this case is basically psychological. A good beginning again as Shiv K. Kumar pointed out in his inaugural speech (not included here), invoking Katherine Mansfield's story 'A Cup of Tea', ensures the reader's participation in the narrative. If the beginning is effective, the middle and end are organically linked to it and to each other. In a sense the end is the beginning, just as the beginning must anticipate the end. The plot of a good short story must have, as Khushwant Singh has pointed out, a curlicue, or a turning point. Premchand's 'The Resignation' has it, as do Narayan's 'Swami and Friends', and Ashokamitran's episode included here from *The Eighteenth Parallel*, a novel which originally appeared as a series of episodes. The rules have mattered because comprehension is basic to enjoyment and criticism. If the Indian short story is now experiencing a boom it is because it has kept the rules in mind, if only to depart from them. The more its departures owe to Indian imperatives, the more the Indian short story will develop and flourish.

A word about the organisation of the papers in the volume. It is obvious that no strict classification of the papers will satisfy because there is so much overlap. Still, the present organisation is based on certain priciples. Since Ashokamitran's contribution speaks for the creative artist it appropriately begins the volume. Vasanthi Sankaranarayanan's essay, while considering some women writers, surveys the development of the Malayalam short story in general and seems appropriate at the point it is placed after Ashokamitran's contribution. The essays by Lakshmi Chandra, Abraham, Santhanam and Sriraman deal with Indian writers in English and are placed in a group. Since Sriraman's article is about English and social class, the transition from it to Mohanty's piece on Fakir Mohan where this issue figures seems natural. Then again Mohanty's paper is on a translated text and is logically followed by essays on translations from Telugu by Keshav, Uma and Sridhar and from Marathi by Marathe. Also, Marathe's paper raises questions about the responsibility of translators in general. With Tutun Mukherjee, who, besides examining translations from Mahasweta Devi, is writing about a premier woman short-story writer, begins the cluster of essays on women writers, comprising those by Ranjana Harish, Murali Manohar and Rekha Pappu. This is followed by Nirmala Nair's paper raising pedagogical issues. The volume is rounded off by S. Viswanathan's summing up that locates the Indian short story in the world of writing in India.

We present this volume in the hope that it will generate more scholarly interest in the subject. In their variety of themes and approaches, points of view and outlook, the essays in this volume hopefully will initiate a debate about the Indian short story and in particular on the continuing role of English in the development of this literary form.

MOHAN RAMANAN
P. SAILAJA

My Writing, My Times

ASHOKAMITRAN

Perhaps I should begin by defining my times before I go on to my writing. I was born sixty-three years ago in a small hospital with six beds in what was then quite a small town, Secunderabad. Secunderabad is today completely surrounded by what is called its twin city, Hyderabad. Hyderabad is the big city and Secunderabad, its little cousin. In 1931 when I was born, the population of Secunderabad was just about eighty thousand, of which less than a thousand were Tamil speaking people. The rest of the population was made up of Telugu and Urdu speaking people. The Tamil people spoke only Tamil but quite a few Telugu families had taken to Urdu and I had seen, in many Telugu families, the father and son or brothers carrying on all interactions in Urdu. Urdu was the state language of Hyderabad State which was also called the Nizam's State. The railway was called the Nizam's State Railway and not the Hyderabad State Railway. The Nizam was the ruler of Hyderabad State just as the Maharajah of Travancore was the ruler of Travancore State or the Maharajah of Mysore was the ruler of Mysore. In those days, school language text books carried a national anthem as the first lesson. It was 'God Save the King.' The second lesson was another anthem, 'God Save the Nizam.' I was puzzled then, as I am now, why they always used the phrase 'God save' in the context of the British king and the Nizam. Some kind of dramatic irony, perhaps.

The first ten or fifteen years of a writer's life provide, in most cases, the bulk of material for his or her writing. My first years were spent in a region where there was a conglomeration of languages, lifestyles, religions, social practices, etc. My father worked for the Nizam's Railway and after nearly twenty years of pleading and cajoling and manoeuvring had managed to get railway quarters, which meant living amongst a community not of one's choice. We had Muslims, Christians, Parsees as our neighbours. A couple of the Christian families were Anglo-Indians. I am not sure about the Railway servants but the families of the Railway servants then were no great lovers of any language. We all spoke our respective languages badly, mixing them with words of any other language that came conveniently to hand. Living in such a heterogeneous community had its advantages as well as disadvantages. The disadvantage was with regard to the rectitude of language, but this was more than made up for by the advantages—a range of experiences and expressions not at all possible in a cohesive, unitary society.

I was just getting to eight when World War II broke out. For six years death and destruction, compounding into a tragedy not easily imaginable for later generations, raged all round India. Technically, India was not a theatre of war, but the impact of war could be felt in almost all aspects of life of the day. Then the Quit India Movement. I was too young to be directly drawn into the war effort or the nationalist movement but I knew I was in the thick of truly momentous days. Soon after the war, Hyderabad faced a special, inconvenient situation. With the British leaving the subcontinent, I suppose it was natural for the rulers of the Princely States to try to be real kings for a while. The war had not eliminated monarchy—there was the King of England, the Queen of Holland, Sultans in the Middle East. Japan continued to have its Emperor who waged a bitter war with the final victors. I suppose the Nizam too fancied becoming a sovereign king. Then there was the question of who would be the ruling class in Hyderabad. The Razakars[1] felt they should be, along with all other Muslims in the state. The whole episode is an awkward, painful one in the history of the last Nizam and his country. In 1948, Hyderabad was merged with the Indian Union and eight years later, the States Reorganisation took away what little was left of the original Hyderabadi way of life. To many who had known the old way of life, this passing away of Hyderabadi culture was received with regret. This is a feeling, I am sure, many people who had lived in the major Princely States of India during the thirties and forties, must have felt. Some of them must have felt quite remorseful.

Anyway, the first twenty years of my life had been in these times and I find the innumerable shades of my experiences in those twenty years colouring the whole body of writing I have done in these forty-odd years. It is quite likely these nuances will go unperceived by a reader today; I can assure him that there is nothing wrong with this—i.e. some undercurrents of a creative work not being realised in their entirety. Can we, after all, be sure we understand every aspect of a work that is created today? But to the writer, these unperceived aspects are quite important, at least, as long as they motivate him to produce more. Again, this also needs to be qualified. Chekhov said that just as there are talking parrots, there are writing parrots. Any motivation can make sense only when it results in meaningful expression. I have in my long life turned out thousands of words and in some way or other, I see them originating from my first twenty years in Secunderabad.

Here in this chapter from my novel *The Eighteenth Parallel* these twenty years seem to unfold—there are many events that will be known as fact, but the organisation of these is what makes it all fiction. I wish to repeat—fiction.

> The impact of 'Vidutalai', the Tamil song on freedom that I sang was beyond all my expectations. The meetings of the Tamil Association of our college used to be the least attended. The Telugu and Urdu Association meetings always found the hall full to overflowing, but the Tamil meetings were mostly addressed to vacant chairs. A few students from other groups would come and sit with us for the first ten or fifteen minutes and then leave. Of the few Tamil-speaking teachers in our college, none except the Tamil pandit came to the Tamil meetings. The Principal, being the president of all College Associations, would adorn the central chair on the dais for five minutes. Not for a moment did I realise that Professor Tambimuthu was among those present when I sang about freedom: 'Vidutalai'. How could I when I was in a state of delirium throughout? Call it ecstasy if you think the word also suggests an uncontrollable tremor of the mind and body.

When Professor Tambimuthu smiled at me, my first thought as usual was that it must be meant for someone else, but it wasn't, Professor Tambimuthu taught us chemistry. I was not on smiling terms with anyone on the staff. In fact, I had become so adept at hiding myself that you could have pointed me out as an exemplar of anonymity. But there were occasions that challenged my claims to anonymity and here was one in the shape of Professor Tambimuthu. That evening found me standing in his room.

'Well, well, you're a Tamil boy, are you?' he said in Tamil and wanted to know my name. Mind you, I had been his student for well over four months. Besides, I had once broken the stopper of the jar containing hydrogen sulphide making the whole class pinch their noses and run. Besides which I also shared my table and cupboard with the only presentable girl in the group. To crown it all, I had made this Tambimuthu himself call me an idiot. Despite all that, I seemed to have somehow managed to keep my name hidden from him. Anyway, I told him my name now.

'I didn't know you could sing,' he said.

My thoughts went back to the Principal of my high school. He had begun the interview in much the same fashion. And then he had gone on to put me on the stage in a saree and had watched the fun.

'What song was that?' Professor Tambimuthu asked.

'Which one sir?'

'The one you sang on Tamil Day.'

'You mean 'Vidutalai' sir?'

'Ah, yes. Say it again.'

'Vidutalai.'

'Sing it now.'

'Here, sir?'

'Yes.'

'Now, sir?'

'Yes now. Is it getting late for you to go home?'

'Yes sir... No sir.'

'Won't take you more than two minutes, my boy. It was wonderful that day, you know.'

'I don't know sir.'

'Now get on with it.'

So I sang 'Vidutalai' in that chemistry room haunted by spirits of Egyptian alchemists and Madame Curie, a curious amalgam altogether.

'Well, write it down for me, will you?'

I blinked as usual. 'Sir, this a Tamil song. It can only be written in Tamil.'

'And you think I don't know Tamil?'

'No sir… All right, sir.'

I tore a sheet from the chemistry practicals notebook and wrote the song down, correcting lines that had sounded wrong when I sang, and in the process spoilt the lines that had been correct. Professor Tambimuthu took the sheet in his hand and scrutinised it.

'May I go now, sir?'

'What's the hurry, sit down.'

I continued to stand. I was afraid he might leave the subject of my singing and move on to my lessons. Also, my thoughts were with *Coverley Papers*, our set text for that year. For some obscure reason, the boys' nickname for Tambimuthu was Will Honeycomb. You may remember that he was the worthless son of a noble family, vain and fond of hunting and women.

'Sing it again,' said the Professor.

'Again, sir?'

'Yes. Again.'

I took the sheet back from him, because I had written my own version of the song in it, and it wouldn't do to change the words while I sang again. This time, he joined me in the singing. I felt uncomfortable. What if somebody should hear our duet? While I sang nervously off-key, the Professor himself didn't seem to be a great believer in sticking to any pitch. So between ourselves, we produced the whole range of sounds that the human voice was capable of. Professor Tambimuthu was extremely happy. I had never imagined that music had such powers. He confessed,

'This is the first time ever that I'm singing a Tamil song.'

'Shall I go now, sir?'

'Wait. Why are you in such a great hurry? Can't you get a bus at this time?'

'I've come by bicycle, sir.'

'That makes it easier still. You can go whenever you please. Now, I'm going to sing the song by myself. See if it's all right.'

And Professor Tambimuthu sang. He explored all those domains of music the rest of us could never have known existed. In the last line of the song each repetition of the thrice repeated word 'Vidutalai' rises higher than the last and I had taught him to strike a really high note at the conclusion. Tambimuthu's voice didn't go very high though his eyeballs kept rolling higher and higher.

Then he asked me proudly, 'Was that all right?'

'Yes sir,' I lied.

'I pick up songs at the first hearing. As for this song, I've been singing it ever since I heard you that day.'

I didn't say anything.

'Whose lyric is this?' he asked.

'Bharati's.'

'Who?'

'Bharati, sir.'

'Who's he? Is he alive now?'

The only thing I knew at that time about the greatest Tamil poet of this century was that *Kalki* magazine had started a collection for a memorial to be built in his name in Ettayapuram, his birthplace. Long lists of donors—several pages of them—were published week after week in this magazine. I knew more about these people than about the poet. My father had donated some money as well, and his name had appeared in the lists. My knowledge of twentieth century Tamil literature was confined to the Tamil weeklies *Ananda Vikatan* and *Kalki* which appeared late in our city. It seemed that Tamil migrants like Tambimuthu had lost even that sort of contact with Tamil. I wondered when his people had migrated to Hyderabad.

So there we were, Tambimuthu and I, in the year of Indian independence, paying homage to our national poet by singing his song of freedom.

'A wonderful song,' said Professor Tambimuthu. 'To

think I wouldn't have known about it, if you hadn't sung it that day.'

'I know two more songs, sir, Actually I had wanted to sing one of the two that day, but they're a bit long.'

'Will you teach them to me?'

'Not today, sir.'

'No. Some other time. And look here.'

'Yes sir.'

'Don't tell anyone.'

I don't know what it was I was not to tell.

'I mean... about my learning the song.'

'All right, sir.' And then I made a big blunder. I said, 'Even Telugu people want to learn this song, sir.'

'I see.... Who?'

'Narasimha Rao sir.'

'Who's Narasimha Rao?'

'A student in the A batch, sir. A Congress leader.'

At the mention of Congress, the Professor's face clouded over.

'Be careful. Don't mix with them.'

'But that may not be possible, sir.'

Professor Tambimuthu stiffened. 'I tell you this because you are a Tamil boy. Don't get mixed up in all this.'

'But I have even given my signature, sir.' I showed him my finger.

'What?'

'We put down our names in blood, sir.'

'What nonsense!'

I took warning. 'Can I go now, sir?'

'What's all this about signatures?'

I stood silent. He won't sing any more freedom songs, I thought.

'What was that about signatures?'

'We've been made to take a pledge, sir.'

'What pledge?' Tambimuthu rebuked me sharply, standing up.

'We are going to demonstrate in front of the College from the first of December.'

'Get out! Get out!'

I darted to the door. But before I was out, the professor called out, 'Chandrasekhar!'

I turned to look at him.

'Come here.'

I went to his table again. He went and closed the door, plunging the darkening room into further darkness. Dusk was falling outside.

'Tell me the whole thing.' I stood determined not to tell him anything, and he sensed it. 'Look, Chandrasekhar,' he said, 'I don't want you to go to the dogs. Let the others do what they like. If there is another strike or demonstration, the trouble-makers will be rusticated.'

I didn't know the exact meaning of 'rustication,' but I knew it must be some sort of punishment.

'Trust me and tell me. It'll stand you in good stead later on.'

My resolve weakened and I told him how I went with Narasimha Rao to meet the leader of the Hyderabad State Congress, that I had been distributing pamphlets among students known to me.

'Do you have any on you now?'

'No sir.'

'What was the pamphlet about?'

I gave him some details. Digambar Rao Bindu had had a meeting with Vallabhbhai Patel in Delhi and it was decided that the college students of Hyderabad should intensify their struggle against the oppression of the Nizam-Razakar combine. The first step was a two-page pledge followed by signatures and there had been fifteen who had signed with me. In blood. I nicked my finger and blood spurted out. Besides me, three other students dipped their pens in my blood and signed. Compared with the pledge written in ink, the names in blood were dim, nearly illegible. Blood didn't seem to be proper material for writing on paper.

I had never seen Professor Tambimuthu in such a sombre mood.

'Were any girls involved?'

'Yes sir. A few. But none from our college.'

'Did you sign because of the girls?'

'Oh no sir. It wasn't like that.'

Professor Tambimuthu stood up. 'I promise not to report this,' he said. 'But I can tell that it's not going to do you any good. Idealism is a good thing, no doubt. Don't I have it myself? Why do you think I learnt this song on freedom from you? Inspiring, indeed. But then, this is no place for idealism. Look at me. I've been in this College for twenty years. Yet, when I asked for a year's leave to go to England, I was asked to resign my job and go. I should have been made the Vice-Principal long ago, but I wasn't even considered for the post. If I recommended a student for a scholarship, he would be the first to be rejected. To survive in this place one must wear a red cap or a turban. Mere cropped heads like me don't get anywhere.' I found it incredible that a chemistry professor should speak so candidly.

'Chandrasekhar, these are trying times,' he went on. 'It's better to complete your studies here in Hyderabad and spend your life here, whether you like it or not. Students from Hyderabad State get no recognition elsewhere. There are no jobs anywhere for them. Hyderabad's merging with India is not going to help you in any way. I know how it is. Nobody outside respects a Hyderabad man. All that's not going to change overnight. Till now we had Englishmen above us; hereafter it will be Gandhi cap people. They're all the same, I tell you, as far as we are concerned, there's no escape for us.' I was afraid he might begin to cry. I came out of the room. It was quite dark outside. Professor Tambimuthu called out from inside the room. 'That wound in your finger, did you put some iodine or something on it? It may get septic.'

Notes

1. The Nizam's guards who terrorised the people of Hyderabad when the Nizam declared himself independent of India in 1947.

The Malayalam Short Story—Evolution, Influences, Original Perspectives

VASANTHI SANKARANARAYANAN

An analysis of the Indian short story (or Malayalam short story) with special emphasis on the influence of English language and literature has to start with the question whether the form of the short story is completely borrowed from the West. Literary critics as well as academics accept the fact that in Indian literary tradition, drama and poetry have indigenous origins. However, prose writing and especially the novel and the short story are considered to be Western products. The novel is undoubtedly a Western form, but, the short story existed in some form or other in the oral tradition of Indian languages. Some examples are *Panchatantra, Kathasaritasagara, Totanama, Aithihyamala*, etc. However, as there has been a break in the short story tradition, especially in the seventeenth, eighteenth, and nineteenth centuries, under British colonial rule, the present Indian short story cannot be realistically traced back to the short story tradition which existed in India before British rule. So, when the short story in India emerged as a literary form in the later years of the nineteenth century and picked up in strength and style, it was only natural to assume that it was fashioned after the Western and especially the English short story. However, in assessing the influence of English on the Indian short story it would be useful to have a break-up of *form* and *content*—form comprising *structure* and *language* and content consisting of *themes* and *concepts*. It would then be clear that while there has been English influence on structure, in terms of content, the short story in India has been uninfluenced or has been only marginally influenced by English or other Western literatures. Even in the matter of concepts, categories like Romanticism, Surrealism, Existentialism, Expressionism, Feminism were not totally unknown in the Indian tradition. They have been used in the poetry and drama of Kalidasa, Bhasa and others though they were not termed as such. So, in looking for the influence of English on the Indian short story, attention has to be focussed on structure and to a certain extent on concepts.

The fact that language in the short story has only been marginally influenced by the West (English) can be proved in two ways. A direct, systematic analysis of the linguistics of English as well as regional languages would prove that the grammar, syntax, and construction of the languages are very different. Such an analysis is not attempted here. An indirect analysis, based on the difficulties encountered in translation from regional languages to English is used to underscore the differences in the two languages. An analysis of these problematic areas shows that the linguistic influence of English on a regional language such as Malayalam is minimal.

The language composition in a Malayalam short story is often through a combination of one word, a few words and full sentences. The single word construction or a combination of a few words in place of the full sentence with the subject-object-verb construction is adopted by many short story writers in order to create a dramatic impact in structure and intensity in emotional portrayals. As examples, I quote 'Brashtu' (Outcaste) by Matampu Kunhukuttan and 'Agni-sakshi' by Lalithambika Antarjanam. The introductory passages in both novels exemplify this. But, if the same structure is adopted in English, the effect is not always dramatic or intense. In translation, the single word or combination construction loses its dramatic impact.

The infusion of the spoken language (as distinguished from the literary language) poses another difficulty in translation. If the spoken language is just a colloquialisation of the literary language, the problem would not be major. But there are dialects and usages specific to regions, communities, religious sections, and castes which are culture-specific and which add new inflections and nuances to the sub-stratum of language. These are very difficult to translate into a language which represents a totally different culture with all its complexities. At best, the received language has to be extended to accommodate these culture-specific usages and dialects. To give a picture of the variety in dialects and usages region-wise, the dialects used by Travancore, Cochin and Malabar (all areas of Kerala) are very different from each other. In the same way, the different communities, such as Namboodiris, Muslims and Christians have their own 'language within language' in the spoken idiom which has made its way into literary works too. Examples are the short stories of Paul Zacharia for the Christian dialect, Vaikkom Muhammad Basheer's short stories for the Muslim dialect and 'Brashtu' referred to earlier for Namboodiri Malayalam. Another dialect is the one arising out of the domination/servility phenomenon, which had forced the lower castes to deliberately use a different (servile) language when addressing their upper caste overlords. For example the use of the word 'atiyan' meaning 'servant' was common when a labourer, addressing a feudal lord, spoke of himself. The lower castes never used the word 'panam' meaning 'money'. They referred to money as 'chempin kasu' meaning 'copper coins'. The humour, the wit and even nuances arising from the dialects and usages of different communities are so specific that without notations and references, it is difficult to convey the individuality of the source text.

Most of the short stories make extensive references to myths, legends, epics, folklore, customs and practices specific to regions, localised religious customs, practices etc. In the source text, these do not pose any problems, as the readers of the region are familiar with all these allusions. In translation, the need for copious notes and references becomes evident. As lengthy explanations cannot be fitted into the text itself for fear of losing the flow and the dramatic impact, these have to be given as footnotes. But too many explanatory footnotes for a short story spoils the flow of the story for the reader and makes it boring. So the translator has to find the right mix and balance when explaining the allusions in the text.

My contention is that apart from the purely linguistic differences in the languages, there are hidden signifiers by way of dialects and culture-specific usages which make it clear that the influence of English on a regional language like Malayalam is very limited.

The main focus of this paper is to critically analyse the generally accepted norm in literary and academic circles that the Indian short story (in this case the Malayalam short story) was influenced in form and content, to a very great extent by the Western (especially English) short story. Dr. K.M. George, an acknowledged authority on the development of Malayalam literature, in his introduction to *Inner Spaces*, an anthology of women's short stories in Malayalam stressed two factors: (a) the short story in Malayalam is quite a developed branch of literature; (b) the impact of the West is clearly visible in the blossoming of the modern short story (George 1993:7). While I agree with his first statement wholeheartedly, his second statement is to be accepted with reservations. Structurally, the Malayalam short story may have been influenced by the classical narrative structure of the West. However, in themes and more importantly, in the language used, which in later days influenced the structure itself, the influence definitely was that of the local dialects, customs, habits, folklore and other cultural contexts. Moreover, in the very use of the spoken as opposed to the literary language, there is clear indication of the regional linguistic traditions. In the women writers, the influence of the regional linguistic tradition is more prominent than that of the Western influence. The women writers, who in the earlier days of the development of the short story had less contact with the Western system of education show greater dependence even in structure on the Indian epics, fables, legends, myths, avoiding the linear narrative structure and adopting a lateral, subjective, epic structure. Emotionally too, they place emphasis on the personal and subjective experiences, and choose styles which suit the narration of these experiences. As women's writing forms a continuum in Malayalam, they can be called in one sense representative of the development of the Malayalam short story. The external influence in the literary tradition of women's writing is limited, partly due to their position in society, which marginalised them and never gave them an opening into mainstream activities such as education, travel, etc., and partly due to their approach to the literary medium as an exploration into their inner spaces, emphasising the personal sphere as the more important one in their lives. As a result, their writing reflects a highly individualistic and indigenous strain. Each of the women authors chosen for study in this paper has a distinct language, style, and conceptualisation. It is very difficult to classify them as part of a movement or trend in literature. But, in retrospect, taken together, they form the hazy, questioning, alternate writing of women, different from the patriarchal mode of writing. In their choice of women as subjects of stories, their compassion for women and their concerns, in expressing a woman's point of view as distinct from a man's point of view, in developing a language which is different from the language of patriarchy, domination and exploitation, they form a distinct genre. This distinct genre is so rooted and culture-specific that the influence of a foreign language and literature is limited.

The writers chosen are Lalithambika Antarjanam and K. Saraswathi Amma (from the thirties and forties), Kamala Das, B. Rajalakshmi and P. Vatsala (from the fifties and sixties), and Sarah Joseph and Manasi (from the modern period).

Antarjanam's short stories reflect a duality: the duality of a woman caught between two types of emotions—the individualistic and the socialistic. The individualistic concerns arise from the caring, nurturing, creative and harmonious instincts of love, compassion and humaneness. The socialistic expressions are aroused by the indignant, reformist, revolutionary ideas couched in protest by the oppressed, exploited community of women. These conflicting emotions prevent her from being aggressively feminist. Professor M. Achyuthan, a well-known critic in Malayalam comments: 'In her desire to unify and extol totally opposing forces and seemingly different emotions, Antarjanam adopts a purely romantic style' (Achyutan 1973:230). This seeming disparity is in itself evidence of a new trend in writing, a hesitantly emerging, alternate women's writing format. What seems to be impossible to combine—humaneness, love and compassion with righteous indignation towards injustice is actualised in Antarjanam's writing. She evolves a form of women's writing which is totally opposed to the injustices perpetrated against women, but hesitates to give up love and tenderness, innate feminine qualities, while fighting for her rights. It is an alternative to the textbook formula of revolutionary protest and social reform which rejects expressions of love and humaneness.

Antarjanam does not follow the same structure in all her short stories. In her two most important stories 'Revenge Herself' and 'The Admission of Guilt' she has used the first person narrative mode. In 'Revenge Herself' the elements of a ghost story are also woven into the structure. This again, can be seen in the light of women's writing. The marginalised woman is basically silenced; her voice is seldom heard; the only way she can make her presence felt is by appearing as a ghost to another concerned and aware woman, a writer, who has the potential to give her a voice through language. Another important story, 'Daughter of Man' adopts a reflective, nostalgic narration. In all these texts, the style is closer to that of a film script, weaving word pictures, using sparse dialogue, moving between time past and time present, giving scope for montage. The stress is on the visual and poetic element in story-telling. It is her rootedness in language and structure and the culture of Kerala that makes her work unique. And in doing so she breaks the linear narrative structure which is a Western construct, combining story, social documentation, narration and visual flashes. Whatever universality of macro-vision she achieves is through her regional identity and micro-vision.

K. Saraswathi Amma, a contemporary of Antarjanam is quite different in her content, style and approach. She too is preoccupied with women's concerns. But, for her, language is only a medium to convey her ideas. Her stories, mostly narratives of a classical mode, have a dramatic suspense, which builds up to a climax, often unexpected. In rare instances, such as 'The Subordinate', she gives an ambiguous and open ending. But, overall, there is a directness in theme and technique. What is amazing in her stories is her avowed denunciation of patriarchy and the uncompromising stances that her protagonists reveal. They do not hesitate to take extreme steps to solve their problems. Saradakutty, the heroine of 'The Soil that Grows Diamonds' deliberately prostitutes herself by marrying an old man to save her family from hunger. Paru Amma, the heroine of 'The Subordinate' kills her daughter so that she won't have to sleep with her father, who did not know of her existence. Through the medium of the short story she constantly strives to uproot patriarchal values and expose their one-sidedness and hypocrisy. In this crusade she undertakes, her tone and style become somewhat propagandistic, strident and rhetorical. 'Her characters are protagonists of her ideology. Beyond that, they do not have any life and vitality' (Achyutan 1973: 234). Saraswathi Amma is again rooted in her language and themes. It is in her concepts that the Western influence is clearly visible. The rising movement of emancipation of women in Europe, England and America and their reflections in literature is evident in Saraswathi Amma.

Kamala Das is very different from other women short story writers in that her style, content and approach to writing are very individualistic, and modern and in some ways not indigenous to Kerala. She reaches out to a sphere of hitherto unexplored ideas and experiences and relates them in a style which is candid and poetic. Her style is not monotonous; she changes her style to suit the theme, ambience and emotional tone of the story. Reading her stories written at different times one cannot make out that they are by the same author. In her children's stories such as 'Summer Vacation', and 'Rice Pudding in Ghee' she goes into the mind and consciousness of a child who has lost his/her mother and carries with him/her an infinite burden of loss and absence. Here her style is simple, direct and very intensely emotional. But her style changes when she is dealing with the man-woman relationship, the frustrations of a monogamous marriage, etc. She is able to adopt the tone of an 'outsider' who reviews the situation detachedly. She often adopts an abstract, psychological, stream of consciousness approach. Her style is never linear, but abstract, evocative, and psychological. Often the poet in her peeps through. She has also written surrealistic stories such as 'Kalyani', 'The Smell of a Bird', and 'Unni' where lost souls seek death as a release from the mechanical and crippling monotony of urban life. Her characters are unusual people who follow their inner instincts and try to unravel their identity. In this attempt they even turn out to be cruel. Kamala Das brings a new language and spirit to the modern Malayalam short story. Though at first sight it may seem to have imbibed a great deal of the external influence of English and Western literature, by its sheer individuality and truthfulness to the modern Indian scenario, it integrates the

Western influence with Indian moorings. In a very complex way it retains its identity as Indian and even Malayali.

B. Rajalakshmi and P. Vatsala who belong to the fifties show very little evidence of the influence of English. Their themes, method of storytelling, the imagery, metaphors, use of the spoken language are all drawn from their local surroundings and milieu. Rajalakshmi adopts a style of thought which is rambling, and not strung together in an organised manner. Vatsala delves into human relationships without adopting a moralising or critical tone. Her language and style change with the theme and ambience of the story. But each theme has a highly individualistic style.

The Modernists, Sarah Joseph and Manasi show a great deal of external influence (be it English or otherwise) in that they do not restrict their stories to any specific Kerala milieu. Often their contexts have a global texture. The language is Malayalam in its evolved form, but it is used to create a new modern, urban language. Conceptually, they resort to surrealism and expressionism. There is no fervour of idealism in their tone, nor do they reflect the utter despair of the disillusioned romantic. They are realists and yet they do not reveal their intentions directly. They move into non-linearity, abstraction and abstruseness with ease. They have moved away from the time-honoured modes of storytelling. They do not propound any ideology. Even their social and political consciousness is couched in their exploration into personal, inner worlds. These are writers in whom the global literary influences are more evident, probably because the boundary lines between countries, languages and cultures are now somewhat blurred. Here again, it is not English literature which is influencing these authors, but world literature. But inasmuch as we get to know world literary works through English translations, there is an indirect influence of English literature.

Works Cited

Achyutan, M. 1973. *Cherukatha Innale, Innu*. Kottayam: Sahityá Pravartaka Cooperative Society Limited.

George, K.M. (ed.). 1993. *Inner Spaces*. New Delhi: Kali for Women.

The Perennial Popularity of R.K. Narayan: An Analysis of 'Father's Help'

LAKSHMI CHANDRA

R.K. Narayan has been writing for more than fifty years and he is as popular today as he was when he started—his novel *The Guide* was made into a movie and his collection of short stories *Swami and Friends* was made into a television serial recently. His writing has been acclaimed by people from all over the world. He has been called 'a man of letters pure and simple' (Srinivasa Iyengar 1962:279) and his language is described as 'pure and limpid... easy and natural' (Walsh 1964:128). Critics have called him 'a conscious craftsman... a master of the art of fiction' (Alam 1994:9) and have noted the 'familiar rhythm, the common and extraordinary rhythm of life' (Walsh 1970:23) that runs through all his work. To what does Narayan owe his perennial popularity? A difficult question to answer, but I think a small contribution towards answering this question has been made in this paper.

In a book entitled *The Narrative Modes* published in 1982, H. Bonheim analyses 600 short stories and 300 novels to arrive at conclusions regarding the devices used in narrative art. He puts forth a model of narrative modes which can be utilised to identify the devices that authors have used. His sample is drawn from British, American and Canadian works. I applied his theory to one of Narayan's short stories ('Father's Help' which is from *An Astrologer's Day and Other Stories*, first published in 1947 and is also found in college anthologies) and the findings are presented in this paper.

Bonheim presents a short history of modes and arrives at four chief narrative modes, which are Description and Comment (these are the static modes where there is no sense of the passing of time), Report and Speech (these are the dynamic modes). He says that each age has its own preferences for particular modes and adds:

> In our own age, speech stands high in the esteem of most readers. Description is thought boring except in small doses; comment of a particular kind, namely moralistic generalising, is almost taboo, even where imbedded in speech; and even report is preferred in the dress of, or at least heavily interlarded with, speech (8).

Bonheim adds a fifth mode, which he calls metanarrative. He says:

> Nor is the model quite absolute in the claim that everything in narrative must belong to one of the four modes. For works of literature contain some elements outside the space/time continuum of the fictional world, including titles, mottoes, prefaces, postscripts, reflections of the author or narrator concerning his literary endeavours, and addresses to the reader. I shall call such elements *metanarrative* (13).

Since this element is not strictly part of the fictional world and since metanarrative is not a popular device in the stories analysed, I have not used it in my analysis of 'Father's Help'.

'Father's Help' is the story of Swami, who like other children of his age, hates going to school. He will do anything, including feigning an illness, to avoid school. Though Mother succumbs to Swami's pretence of illness, Father is more stern. Swami then lies about his teacher Samuel, who is supposed to beat children till they bleed. Father, unfortunately, believes this lie and sends Swami to school with a letter to the headmaster complaining about Samuel. The story ends on an ironic note, which will be discussed later in this paper.

An analysis of 'Father's Help' reveals that most of the story is told in the form of dialogue, of speech, interspersed with report. The description is limited to a few sentences within the speech or report. There are no chunks of descriptive paragraphs. The comments made are negligible. Narayan's preference for the dynamic modes is obvious, a preference which readers today share.

Bonheim also looks at the use of inquits—speech tags or reporting phrases like 'he said,' 'she replied'—in his sample fiction. There are three positions for the inquit:

- at the beginning, as in 'Ram said, "Let's go to the movies."'
- in the middle, as in '"Go home," said Mother, "and be quick about it."'
- at the end, as in '"The meeting is scheduled for tomorrow," said the Manager.'

Bonheim's analysis reveals that modern writers prefer to do away with this device wherever possible (the zero stage), and if necessary, use it at the end of the sentence. In the fifteenth century there was a strong preference for inquits in the initial position, at the beginning—in William Caxton's *Paris & Vienne* (1485), the initial inquit occurs 98 per cent of the time. This is contrasted with Paul Scott's *A Division of the Spoils* (1975), where the preference for an inquitless narrative is predominant—64 per cent. In modern narrative, speech follows speech without any interruptions. The readers are able to distinguish a change in the speaker with the help of crypto-inquits. These are 'hidden' markers of speech of different speakers who might speak different dialects. A change of pronouns, or viewpoints or subject matter also alert the readers to the change in the speaking voice. All these are crypto-inquits. An analysis of 'Father's Help' reveals Narayan's preference for inquitless narrative too—the percentage is similar to Scott's—64 per cent—another reason for the modern reader's partiality towards Narayan.

Let us now turn our attention to short story beginnings. For short story writers, the opening is especially important. This opening is a composite of many things. It is at the beginning that the author has to set the tone of the story, describe the setting and the protagonist, and give the time during which any action takes place. Due to its brevity, the distinguishing feature of this genre, the structure has to be tightly knit and the opening plays an important part.

Of the four narrative modes, Comment has been avoided as an opening device—only 5 per cent of the stories surveyed opened with Comments. Description (35 per cent) and Report (31 per cent for pre-1990 and 49 per cent for post-1900) are the most popular modes used to begin a short story. Though there is a preference for the dynamic modes, Speech is not popularly used for openings—only 11 per cent of the stories surveyed used Speech. The survey shows the main difference between pre- and post-1900 fiction—the preference for Report in post-1900 fiction leading to the overall preference for the dynamic modes. Here is the table from Bonheim (191):

Statistical Survey of Narrative Modes in the Short Story

	Anglo-American						*Canadian*		*Anglo-American and Canadian together*	
	Pre-1900		*Post-1900*		*Together*					
Short Story beginnings										
Metanarrative	13	12%	2	1%	15	5%	13	4.3%	28	5%
Comment	15	13%	7	4%	22	7%	10	3.3%	32	5%
Description	40	36%	64	34%	104	35%	124	41.3%	228	38%
Report	35	31%	92	49%	127	42%	113	38.0%	240	40%
Speech	9	8%	23	12%	32	11%	36	12.0%	68	11%
Uncertain							4	1.0%	4	1%
Sum	112	100%	188	100%	300	100%	300	100.0%	600	100%

Now let us look at the opening paragraph of 'Father's Help':

> Lying in bed, Swami realised with a shudder that it was Monday morning. It looked as though only a moment ago it had been the last period on Friday; already Monday was there. He hoped that an earthquake would reduce the school building to dust, but that good building—Albert Mission School—had withstood similar prayers for over a hundred years now. At nine o'clock Swaminathan wailed: 'I have a headache.' His mother said: 'Why don't you go to school in a jutka?'
>
> (Narayan 1964:125)

The easiest mode to identify is Speech and that, we can see, is used at the end of the paragraph. Description can be of time, place or person. When the person begins to move, that Description becomes Report. Report is marked by the use of action verbs, the past tense, especially the past perfect tense, and the use of time-markers. Comments are like 'asides' in drama, generalisations, usually abstract, not made by any of the characters of the story. Using this framework, an analysis of Narayan's opening paragraph shows the use of Report, mixed with Speech, with a modicum of description and comment. Once again, Narayan's preference for report as an opening mode corresponds with the trends in modern twentieth century fiction, adding to the reason for his popularity even today.

How do modern authors end their stories? Let us look at some of the techniques used to end short stories. These are:

- the death or disappearance of the protagonist
- the repetition of something from the beginning of a story, maybe even the title
- a shift in the diction from formal to informal or vice versa
- a deviation from the norm in syntax, i.e. use of inverted, elaborated or fragmentary syntax
- the use of similes
- the use of irony
- the brevity of the final sentence (five words or less).

These techniques are used along with the four modes. In pre-1900 fiction, Comment and Description accounted for 42 per cent of the endings whereas the figure is just 26 per cent for post-1900 fiction. Report is equally popular in both—26 per cent for pre-1900 and 30 per cent for post-1900 fiction. The marked difference comes in the use of Speech, which from 19 per cent in pre-1900 fiction doubled to 38 per cent in post-1900 fiction. Here is Bonheim's table for short story endings (191):

Statistical Survey of Narrative Modes in the Short Story

	Anglo-American						*Canadian*		*Anglo-American and Canadian together*	
	Pre-1900		*Post-1900*		*Together*					
Short Story beginnings										
Metanarrative	11	10%	2	1%	13	4%	9	3%	22	4%
Comment	27	24%	25	13%	52	17%	42	14%	94	26%
Description	20	18%	24	13%	44	15%	49	16%	93	15.3%
Report	29	26%	57	30%	86	29%	96	32%	182	30%
Speech	21	19%	72	38%	93	31%	97	32%	190	32%
Uncertain	4	4%	8	4%	12	4%	7	2%	19	3%
Sum	112	100%	188	100%	300	100%	300	100%	600	100%

Now let us look at the concluding paragraph of 'Father's Help':

> Swami held up the envelope and said: 'I will give this to the headmaster as soon as he is back...' Father snatched it from his hand, tore it up, and thrust it into the waste-paper basket under his table. He muttered: 'Don't come to me for help even if Samuel throttles you. You deserve your Samuel...' (133).

First, let's analyse the techniques Narayan uses. The story ends on an ironic note—the headmaster is on leave and the acting headmaster is none other than Samuel, Swami's teacher! Swami runs home with the incriminating letter. Father, of course, does not believe Swami, and therefore, the ironic tone in the last few sentences. The use of fragmentary syntax is depicted in the last sentence, which is also a very brief sentence—only four words. Modern authors tend to use epanalepsis in a very subtle way and this is what Narayan does—the title of the story is 'Father's Help' and this idea is repeated when *Father* says, 'Don't come to *me* for *help* even if Samuel throttles you' (emphasis mine). These techniques are combined with Report and Speech with which Narayan ends his story. This again, is a modern technique likely to appeal to readers of today.

Endings can also be divided into closed and open endings. Closed endings are those where the author signals to the reader, using the various techniques mentioned earlier, that the end of the story is at hand. Open endings are those which do not use these signals, where action and dialogue are used to the very end, where conflicts are left unresolved and action suspended rather than concluded. The preference today, is towards the open ending. A word of caution—the line of demarcation between open and closed endings is difficult to draw and the terms 'more' or 'less' are usually applied along with these absolute terms, e.g. 'more closed' or 'more open'. Another term which has been used is the 'Janus-headed ending' which 'combines the final look back which is essential to the closed endings... with the sugestion that life goes forward which is essential to the open one' (Bonheim: 143). I feel this is the perfect term to be applied to most modern short stories. Another look at Narayan's closing paragraph reveals that this is what Narayan does—he uses the

Janus-headed ending. He uses quite a few techniques to signal the ending, but we get a sense of life moving on, of there being no resolution to the action. Dialogue is used till the very end. This is a modern technique and another reason for Narayan's popularity with readers.

This story was written in English and is not a translation. Therefore the techniques used are, undoubtedly, the author's own. Let us also remember that this story was first published in an anthology in 1947. Even today children can easily identify themselves with the protagonist Swami. They can applaud his antics and sympathise with his predicament. They may even use similar techniques to stay out of school! The adults find themselves identifying with the protagonist too—maybe thinking about the past and the tricks they used not to go to school. This story shows how Narayan is able to feel the pulse of the people around him and how he is able to identify universal truths that do not lose their appeal, regardless of the passage of time. In other words, he knows how to universalise experience. This is why this story stands up favourably to criticism which is based on theory published in 1982. This also testifies to the fact that R.K. Narayan has a feel for the English language, and an innate ability to write fiction which cannot be dated, fiction which can appeal to readers anywhere. This is the reason that the academic community all over the world has acclaimed him as 'a writer who transcends the regional and national barriers and writes (though almost always about India and from an Indian perspective) about mankind and for readers everywhere' (Mcleod 1994:v).

Works Cited

Alam, Fakrul. 1994. 'Narrative Strategies in Two Narayan Novels.' *R.K. Narayan: Critical Perspectives*. New Delhi: Sterling Publishers.

Bonheim, Helmut. 1982. *The Narrative Modes*. Cambridge: D.S. Brewer.

Mcleod, A.L. (ed.). 1994. *R.K. Narayan: Critical Perspectives*. New Delhi: Sterling Publishers.

Narayan, R.K. 1964. 'Father's Help.' *An Astrologer's Day and Other Stories*. Mysore: Indian Thought Publications.

Srinivasa Iyengar, K.R. 1962. *Indian Writing in English*. Bombay: Asia Publishing House.

Walsh, William. 1964. *A Human Idiom: Literature and Humanity*. London: Chatto and Windus.

—. 1970. *A Manifold Voice: Studies in Commonwealth Literature*. London: Chatto and Windus.

When East is West: A Thematic and Stylistic Analysis of Bharati Mukherjee's *The Middleman and Other Stories*

P.A. ABRAHAM

The short story is the perfect literary form to win swift recognition of excellence and appreciation. In fact the art of the short story demands a conscious awareness. It is impressionistic and does not depend on structure or plot, but on swiftly perceived design. According to H.E. Bates (1941:16), a short story writer is the freest of all artists in words. To quote him:

> The short story whether short or long, poetical or reported, plotted or sketched, concrete or cobweb, should have an insistent and eternal fluidity that slips through the hands.

Every detail in a story must add to its oneness or wholeness. It demands a high degree of compression and concentration. Like poetry, a short story maintains a sustained effect. According to Thomas Gullason '...most modern short story writers are agreed that their medium is closer to poetry than to the novel' (Gullason 1964:129). For such a writer as Bharati Mukherjee, who has also written novels, the short story would seem a natural medium, for expressing her thoughts concisely, not wasting a single sentence or detail.

This paper is an attempt to explore the immigrant sensibility as depicted in Bharati Mukherjee's *The Middleman and Other Stories* (1989), to see how well she has adopted the short story form to capture the energy of a country (America), its people, and its language by discovering a style of writing, native to America, that has pace, vigour and urgency.

Unlike her characters in the earlier books, the people in this collection of short stories are brave, ambitious and sometimes reckless. They dream big and in the process of realising their dreams, abandon centuries of tradition, morality and inhibition. Coming from what Mukherjee calls 'nothing places', they have made America their 'New World'. Through these stories Mukherjee tries to delineate the manner in which these energetic and diverse immigrants are altering the face of America. It is with this collection that Mukherjee's genius has truly flowered. She has, from an immigrant, turned 'unhyphenated' American. Thus, the new changing America is the theme of the stories in *The Middleman.* For Mukherjee, immigration from the Third World to America is a metaphor for the process of uprooting and rerooting or what her husband Clark Blaise in his book *Resident Alien* calls 'unhousement' and 'rehousement'. In an interview with Alison B. Carb (1990:33), Mukherjee points out:

> The immigrants in my stories go through extreme transformation in America and at the same time they alter the country's appearance and psychological make-up. In some ways they are like European immigrants of earlier eras. But they have different gods. And they come for different reasons.

In the title story, Alfie Judah, the narrator of the story is the middleman who travels around the world providing people with guns, narcotics and automobiles. The story takes place in an unnamed country in Central America where Alfie becomes involved in guerilla warfare. Maria, the dark, sensuous, liberated Latin woman is yet another character in the story who deserves attention. She has a number of affairs including a passionate sexual encounter with Alfie who has a weakness for women. She is involved in guerilla warfare, kills her current husband Clovis Ransome and goes away with Andreas, her former lover, a husky revolutionary. Alfie could also have been killed by her. But, according to him:

> She has made love to me three times tonight. With Andreas

> today, doubtless more. Never has a truth been burned so deeply in me, what I owe my life to, how simple the rules of survival are... (Mukherjee 1989:21).

In a flashback, the situation in a sexually free society like America and an orthodox society like Iraq are juxtaposed. Here Alfie remembers that when he was a child in Iraq, he had been taken to witness a young, beautiful woman being stoned to death in public for adultery.

The story involves the reader in a new experience, where he is able to capture human relationships which establish levels of meaning and weave them into intricate patterns leading to a significant insight into the 'human condition'.

In 'A Wife's Story', Panna Butt, who has come to the U.S. on a scholarship casts her mind over the past as she rides in a cab in New York with her Russian lover Imre. Then, there is an unexpected visit from her husband, a textile executive in Ahmedabad. The resulting sexual episodes show that the new land has transformed her unalterably as she watches her naked body in the mirror:

> I stand here shameless, in ways he has never seen me. I am free, afloat, watching somebody else (4).

In the story, 'Loose Ends', a Vietnam war veteran Job Marshall, narrates his story in Miami where he drives into the dark parking lot of the Dunes Motel:

> Inside in a room reeking of incense are people eating. There are a lot of them. There are a lot of brown people sitting cross-legged on the floor of a regular motel room and eating with their hands. Pappies with white beards, grannies swaddled in silk, men in dark suits, kids, and one luscious jailbait in blue jeans. They look at me. A bunch of aliens and they stare like I'm the freak (52).

So he is to them but we know that the owners are Indians and that Mukherjee is making a point with some subtlety that to them Marshall may be just as freakish. In the event, Marshall, who is given to acting first and then thinking, rapes the Indian girl who has a certain dignity, before he gets his work done.

In 'Orbiting' a New Jersey woman of Italian origin invites her parents and her Afghan boyfriend Ro to a Thanksgiving dinner at her home, and a crisis begins over who should carve the turkey—her father or her boyfriend. This cross-cultural conflict is a common theme in Mukherjee's stories, and is often a source of comedy, that leads on to misunderstandings and then to anger and violence. In this story, however, the Afghan boy, who has moved from airport to airport for refuge from his country's battle-fields, 'brings out his dagger... and slashes and slices, swiftly, confidently at the huge browned juicy turkey breast'.

The girl concludes:

> I am seeing Ro's naked body as though for the first time, his nicked, scarred, burned body. In his body the blemishes seem embedded, more beautiful like wood... I am seeing character made manifest... If I trace the puckered tissue on his left thigh and ask 'How Ro?' he becomes shy. He's ashamed that he comes from a culture of pain (74).

In 'The Tenant', Maya Sanyal divorced from an American husband after two years, has become American enough to say that she 'has slept with married men, with nameless men, with men little more than boys, but never with an Indian man' (103).

She is having an affair with her latest landlord, a handless man (a new experience) after a blind date. The reader follows breathlessly the twists and turns in Maya Sanyal's thinking as she agonises over whether she should finally decide to let go of the old ways and world or whether she should live the twilight life of the 'reluctant' immigrant. In the final analysis, she decides that she will no longer remain in 'ideal space' and take the leap (mind, body and soul) into the new land.

'Jasmine' is the story of a girl named Jasmine who comes from Port of Spain, Trinidad, illegally and eventually makes love to her employer, for whom she works as an *au pair* girl while his wife is away. For her, it is probably an induction to the American ethos as well. Here, once again, Mukherjee uses her protagonist's sexual escapades to symbolise her realisation that she is not the 'Flower of Trinidad' but the 'Flower of Ann Arbor'. Although the denouement in this story seems inevitable, it is not the fact that Jasmine succumbed to her American employer that is important, but it is where the act of seduction transports her that is crucial:

> She felt so good she was dizzy. She'd never felt this good on the island where men did this all the time, and girls went along with it always for favours. You could not feel really good in a nothing place (138).

At this special moment, Jasmine realises that in America alone, she is her own person.

In 'Danny's Girls' Danny Sahib is a 20 year old Dogra boy from Simla, sizzling with ambition to make it in a greedy town called Flushing. He thinks on a mega scale and defies both the law and the Indian attitudes. He is not in the New World to become a mere scientist or engineer when the big money lies in working scams. So, he sets up a 'marriage business' which freely translated, means selling 'docile Indian girls to hard up Indian American boys' (143).

Danny decides to liberate himself from old world morals in order to establish himself in the New World. Danny Sahib may have gone through a process of 'unhousement' when he left his hometown in the sylvan hills of Simla. But, by claiming tenancy over the social mores of his new home in Flushing, New York, he 'rehouses' himself. While Jasmine's guiltlessness is one form of freedom which America provides, Danny Sahib's ability to make easy money is another.

The stories show that Mukherjee's is a world of violence and quick transitions and transformation for the uprooted individual. She tells the stories of these people without any inhibitions, leaving the reader sometimes exhausted, sometimes frightened, but always impressed by her simple, terse and matter-of-fact language, which is, in fact, the chief unifying factor within which the stories exist. In all these stories Mukherjee has adopted a style that is colloquial, unvarnished and functional, based on the oral narrative pattern. The title story in *The Middleman* begins as follows:

> There are only two seasons in this country, the dusty and the wet. I already know the dusty and I'll get to know the wet (3).

Here, the reader is at once taken to a different land and a sort of curiosity is aroused from the beginning. The language used by Mukherjee is straight-forward and uninhibited. The narrator of the story says: 'I must confess my weakness... It's woman' (4). In 'A Wife's Story', the predicament of an immigrant is depicted in lucid language:

> English isn't his best language. A refugee from Budapest, he has to listen hard... It's the tyanny of the American dream that scares me. First, you don't exist. Then you're invisible. Then you're funny. Then you're disgusting. The insult, my American friends will tell me, is a kind of acceptance (26).

In 'The Tenant' when Maya introduces herself saying 'Call me Maya' (102), the reader is ready to hear her story immediately.

Sometimes, Mukherjee uses parody to depict the kind of English used by Indians. To cite an example, in 'A Wife's Story' (40) when the husband talks to the wife about a phone call he receives from India, he says:

> What is this woman saying?... I am not understanding these Negro people's accents.

The tendency to use the progressive present tense when the simple present tense is required, is an example of an 'Indianism' in the story. Earlier, the narrator says:

> My husband sends me in to buy the tickets, because he has come to feel Americans don't understand his accent (35).

By depicting the problem of language Mukherjee indirectly suggests that an immigrant/newcomer is often caught between two cultures and languages and is made to negotiate a new social space in an alien country.

In order to achieve the desired effect, Mukherjee, in her stories, has employed both dramatic and narrative methods. The advantage of the dramatic method is the vividness of illusion it creates. This method also gives pleasure by putting the reader to work. Mark the following passage from the story 'The Tenant' (111) which shows the successful combination of the dramatic and the narrative:

> And I, she wants to ask, do I tempt?
> 'Now tell me about yourself, Maya.'
> He makes it easy for her.

> 'Have you ever been in love?'
> 'No.'
> 'But many have loved you, I can see that.' He says it not unkindly. It is the fate of women like her and men like him. Their karmic duty, to be loved. It is expected not judged. She feels he can see them all, the sad parade of need and demand. This isn't the time to reveal all. And so the courtship enters a second phase.

The stories have pace, violence, sex and a language sometimes amounting for us in India to jargon, and Mukherjee claims that it is American.

> ... and I watch her corkscrew to her feet. I'm so close. I can hear her ligaments pop (8).

Or, to cite an example from 'Jasmine':

> They'd gotten here before the rush and bought up a motel and an ice-cream parlour. Jasmine felt very superior when she saw Mr. Daboo in the motel's reception area. He was a pumpkin-shaped man with very black skin and Elvis Presley sideburns turning white (128).

This experimentation with the natural rhythms of American speech has become a major stylistic characteristic of Mukherjee.

Mukherjee's use of imagery and symbols also evokes a variety of feelings and emotions. In order to create atmosphere and intensify violence, the writer also uses the heroine's irresistible sex appeal:

> Her long thighs press and squeeze. She tries to hold me, to contain me, and it is a moment I would die to prolong. In a frenzy, I conjugate crabs with toads and the squawking bird, and I hear the low moans of turtles on the beach. It is a moment I fear too much..., and I yield. I begin again immediately, this time concentrating on blankness, on burnt-out objects whirling in space (18–19).

In 'Orbiting', the narrator states:

> Rindy, all night I've been up and awake. All night I think of your splendid breasts. Like a cluster of grapes. I think I am stroking and fondling your grapes this very minute (66).

However, Mukherjee does not seem to suggest that sex is an antidote to human loneliness and suffering. The above quoted passage from 'The Middleman' suggests the ultimate human predicament of loneliness. While 'conjugating crabs with toads', 'the squawking bird', and 'the low moans of turtles on the beach' suggest sexual energy and desire, 'blankness' and 'burnt-out objects whirling in space' suggest the emptiness of life.

In these stories Mukherjee fulfils the dictum of short fiction to tell little but suggest much. She selects the small moment which is a keyhole to an entire revelation. To suggest, to hint, to imply but not to state directly or openly—this is one of Mukherjee's methods of telling her story. This method is well described by L.A.G. Strong (1934:281–82):

> Instead of giving us a finished action to admire or pricking the bubble of some problem he [the short story writer] may give us only the key-piece of a mosaic, around which if sufficiently perceptive, we can see in shadowy outline the completed pattern.

It is not directly stated why Maria, Panna Bhatt, Charity Chin or Maya Sanyal behave the way they do. Have they chosen their way voluntarily? Or are they victims of circumstances? All this is left to the imagination of the readers.

Technically, the stories range rather freely and widely in time, space and point of view, and they pass through tense moments. All through one is struck by the tautness and effectiveness of Mukherjee's language which is a model of lucidity and flexibility. H.L. Mencken once wrote that American English has largely rid itself of density and freight in the interests of mobility. According to him it 'cultivates a grammar of transit, not of memories of inheritance'. In other words, it is a language that suits the speeding lives of Mukherjee's characters. And, more important, it is a language that she has grasped; she is 'inventing' the American landscape and 'repossessing' the American language, making it her own.

From the language to the actual characters themselves the two are so inextricably intertwined that they speak to us as one, the hallmark of truly great writing. In story after story the great ease that Mukherjee displays with her subject and idiom draws the reader right in.

However, like other immigrant writers, Mukherjee also cannot extricate herself entirely from her past traditions. She has to carry these traditions with her, her 'collective unconscious' which must be reinterpreted by the mainstream culture and must in turn revitalise the culture she meets headlong. It is again in the matter of language—of adopting the English language as a medium of expression to convey Indian thought and sensibility—that some of her stories have acquired a flavour of their own. For instance, in her story 'Wife', Mukherjee uses the word 'mangalasutra' for the marriage necklace the wife wears while going to receive her husband at the airport. The whole scene takes the reader back to Indian traditions and customs. She is also fond of using Indian names like Patel, Kusum, Panna Bhatt, Kantilal Shah, Jasmine and many others in her stories.

A feminist reading of the text shows that Mukherjee is in quest of a body experienced by women as subject of their desires and not as object of man's desires. The women characters in Mukherjee's stories—Maria in 'The Middleman', Panna Bhatt, and Charity Chin in 'A Wife's Story', Maya Sanyal in 'The Tenant' and others live according to their own terms. They are liberated from the shackles of the patriarchal system. In 'The Middleman', at the end Andreas looks at Maria as though to say 'You decide'. Again it is the language used by Mukherjee that establishes women's power:

> She holds out her hand and Andreas slips the pistol in it. This seems to amuse Clovis Ransome. He stands presenting an enormous target. 'Sweetie'—he starts and she blasts away and when I open my eyes he is across the bed sprawled in the far corner (20–21).

Here, Mukherjee questions the dominant literary tradition suggesting like Sheila Rowbotham (1973:33) that,

> Language is part of the political and ideological power of the rulers. We can't just occupy existing words. We have to change the meaning of words even before we take them over.

Through these stories Mukherjee tries to prove that if a woman is to write she must deconstruct the self that is a 'male opus' and discover a living inconstant self. She must in Bloomian terms, replace the 'imitation' with 'originality', rejecting and replacing crippling patriarchal prescriptions.

Mukherjee's growth as a writer is that she no longer limits herself to Indian immigrants, but to the whole of the developing world. The easy familiarity extends to native Americans as well, for half of the stories in *The Middleman* are narrated by them. Her characters do not ask for our sympathy nor are they plunged into doom, gloom and nostalgia. They are trying to carve a niche for themselves. But it is not sure if they really get a share of the American pie in return.

There are many levels within the stories which provide the reader a collective experience of America. At a simplistic level, the author includes the sheer geographic scale of the nation by placing her stories across a vast territory from Ann Arbor in the North to Atlanta in the South.

At a more metaphorical level, the stories move at a high speed, to keep in time with America's jet-set pace. The reader has difficulty keeping track of characters who act fast, hustling careers and life styles.

A reader's initial reaction to these stories may be almost negative. But Mukherjee's style is consistent with the mood and setting of the stories, where she has demonstrated an admirable visual sense, an ability to compose a scene or to evoke a person, place or thing memorably with a few carefully sketched details. The final effect of all these is a haunting quality of evocation that pervades her stories.

In the portrayal of her characters and through the use of language, Mukherjee presents a new vision of the immigrants in America. They broaden the perspective of America presented to the reader by authors such as John Updike and John Cheever. Updike and Cheever are concerned with the crisis of mainstream Americans—divorce, drugs, mid-life dilemmas and the perils of suburbia. Mukherjee's is a world populated by Asian immigrants who in fact, have no cultural framework from which to draw common experience, no code of manners by which to initiate, guide and sustain meaningful relationships among individuals. Though they appear to be characters full of life, enjoying a new sense of liberation, they are, in fact, lonely, confused and anxious. Through the subtle art of evocation and suggestion Mukherjee tries to convey this sense of loss experienced by the immigrants. If one reads Mukherjee's stories for their moral implication or as a guide to life, one is likely to be disappointed, for in that sense they do not tell us enough. But there is another more fruitful way of reading her stories, i.e. they can be read as an expression of a sensitive witness to the national/immigrant experience.

Works Cited

Bates, H.E. 1941. *The Modern Short Story*. London: Nelson and Sons.

Carb, Alison. 1990. 'Bharati Mukherjee: The Immigrant Sensibility— An Interview'. *Span*. XXXI:b. June.

Gullason, Thomas A. 1964. 'The Short Story: An Underrated Art', *Studies in Short Fiction*. 6, Fall.

Mukherjee, Bharati, 1989. *The Middleman and Other Stories*. New York: Penguin.

Rowbotham, Sheila. 1973. *Woman's Consciousness, Man's World*. Harmondsworth: Penguin.

Strong, L.A.G. 1934. 'The Short Story: Notes at Random'. *Lovet Dickson's Magazine*. II March.

The Immigrant Sensibility in Bharati Mukherjee's *The Middleman and Other Stories*

K. SANTHANAM

Bharati Mukherjee is one of the important Third-World writers to have won international recognition in recent times. Born in Calcutta in 1940 in a traditional Bengali family and married in 1960 to Clark Blaise, a creative writer in Canada, she became a Canadian citizen. Her seven years' stay in Canada made her feel like an 'alienated outsider' and an unwanted 'visible minority' (Hancok 1987:301). The racial discrimination meted out to the expatriates in Canada made her leave that country. She came to the U.S.A. in 1980 to become a permanent citizen there.

Though she has a few novels to her credit like *The Tiger's Daughter*, *Wife* and *Jasmine*, recognition came to her with the 1988 National Book Critics award for *The Middleman and Other Stories*. *The Middleman* presents a fascinating account of the experiences encountered by the immigrants who come to settle permanantly in America. F.A. Inamdar quotes Mukherjee's remark: 'We immigrants have fascinating tales to relate… My aim is to expose Americans to the energetic voices of the new settlers in this country' (Inamdar 1991:187). Mukherjee writes about the immigrants who come from diverse countries and cultures with a vision of the American dreamland; they merge themselves completely into the American 'melting pot' resulting in a complete transformation of identity. These protagonists not only reject their inherited cultural values and traditions but also embrace the new American values and ethos totally, so that they become part of mainstream American culture.

This paper proposes to examine *The Middleman and Other Stories* in terms of the American experience of the immigrant characters. This American experience refers to the appropriation of the typical American socio-cultural values by these immigrants: socio-cultural values like leading an uninhibited sex life, and resorting to violence and murder which have almost become part and parcel of American social life. This appropriation of the American socio-cultural ethos results in the complete transformation of their character and identity. The immigrant experience of these protagonists involves a two-way process, 'a process of unhousement' and 'rehousement' (Hancok 1987:290). 'Unhousement' refers to breaking away from the culture into which one has been born and brought up. 'Rehousement' refers to the re-rooting of oneself in a new culture. This two-way process results in the complete transformation of one's personality or self in terms of acquired culture and traditions. Bharati Mukherjee is fascinated by these new immigrants who have 'indomitable will, energy and ambition to pull out of their roots and so her stories are about conquests and not about loss' (Hancok: 295). Her collection of stories presents a realistic account of the problems and the difficulties encountered by these immigrants during their process of adjustment in coming to terms with the values of the new dreamland of their choice. Many of the immigrants, especially from the Third World want to settle permanently in America by taking up a position. America lures them with the promise of a new land with plenty of opportunities to lead a rich and comfortable life.

Some of the stories delineate the physical and mental suffering these prospective immigrants have to go through to reach their final destination. Thus 'Buried Lives' narrates the story of the middle-aged school teacher Venkatesan who decides to leave Sri Lanka after his terrible experience with the Tamil Tigers and, his own part in killing a Buddhist monk. He succeeds in getting a fake passport through a middleman by paying a huge sum of money which would ensure him a safe passage to Germany. He takes a circuitous route from Sri Lanka via India and Russia to Berlin. On his arrival in Berlin he is taken to Hamburg by an

Algerian in a truck. He is accommodated in a cheap motel meant for undocumented transients where he is exposed to filthy language used by the inmates of the place.

'A Wife's Story' narrates the story of an Indian girl, Panna, hailing from a traditional Gujarati family and married to a mill owner in Ahmedabad. On her arrival in America she makes love to Imre, an Asian settled in America. Her short stay in America makes her so completely Americanised, that she is able to take a lover Imre, and even hug him in public. Even Imre is surprised at her unexpected behaviour. Panna takes pride in the fact that her horizons have broadened, and she realises that this would not have been possible had she not left her home. Like the narrator herself, Panna undergoes a complete transformation in her new life: 'Part of my life is over', she says, 'the way trucks have replaced lorries in my vocabulary' (Mukherjee 1990:32).

The full force of the author's irony is revealed when Panna takes her husband who is on a short visit to the U.S. on an American tour. Her roommate Charity Chin, 'interested in hand-modelling, has had her eyes fixed eight or nine months ago and out of gratitude sleeps with her plastic surgeon every third Wednesday' (39). Charity too is also fully Americanised. When she first moved in she was seeing an analyst. Now she sees a nutritionist. Estranged from her husband Eric, she is having an affair with Phil, a flautist 'who has thin hair'. She spends the weekends with him riding in his Datsun.

Though Panna is completely transformed she displays a superficial attachment to Indian tradition: she wears a saree when she goes to JFK airport to meet her husband, and she does not forget to wear her marriage necklace, the mangalasutra.

'The Tenant' tells us the story of a fully liberated Indian woman hailing from Calcutta, Maya Sanyal, now settled in the U.S.A. When we meet Maya for the first time, we see her sitting at the kitchen table drinking bourbon. She had been maried to an American, John, who divorces her. Though now she stays with Fran, she has not told him about her past except that she is a divorcee. She takes pride in the fact she has slept with married men, with nameless men, but never with an Indian man. She now responds to the marriage advertisement by Ashok Mehta, an Indian settled in the U.S.A. though she has not disclosed her past. Mehta learns that Maya is not free of problems. But her new life-style, her sleeping with unmarried men does not deter him from entering into a marital relationship with her. 'It is the fate of women like her and men like him. Their karmic duty to be loved. It is expected not judged' (111). Maya now makes advances to Fred, a man without arms, who is already married, though at the same time she has fond hopes of marrying Ashok Mehta. Bharati Mukherjee ironically says that this is how immigrant courtship proceeds. This story clearly shows how the immigrants coming to America try to assimilate into the mainstream of American values by repudiating their age-old, inherited customs and traditions.

'Jasmine' tells us the story of a girl, Jasmine, from Port of Spain, Trinidad, who taks a circuitous journey via Canada to reach Detroit, U.S.A. Jasmine is a girl with an ambition. She takes up all kinds of jobs like book-keeping, and cleaning and thus emerges as a real survivor. She becomes a housemaid in Bill Moffit's house and slowly she begins to throw her weight around. She wants to pursue a course at the University of Michigan in Ann Arbor with the help of Bill Moffit. Her intimacy with the Moffits helps her to establish deeper roots in America. At the end of the story, her transformation is so complete with her sexual initiaton with Bill, that she becomes the flower of Ann Arbor and not of Trinidad. This story shows how a girl from Trinidad is completely absorbed both in letter and spirit into American culture and ethos.

'The Middleman' presents the story of Alfie Judah, the middleman. He himself confesses that he has a weakness for women. Now he works for Clovis T. Ransome and has a sexual affair with Ransome's wife Maria. When Maria was fourteen years of age and about to be married to the guerrilla insurgency leader, Andreas, she was taken away by Gutterez, the Minister of Education, who visited her school. Now she expects Alfie to take her away from Clovis. When Maria sees Andreas, she throws herself on him and he holds her face in his hands and 'in no time they are swaying and moaning like connubial visitors at a prison farm' (30). Andreas and Maria visit Ransome, rob him of his money and Maria kills him with Andreas' gun. No true love exists between husband and wife. Here is a classic example of a wife murdering her husband for survival. Maybe poor Alfie saves his life because Maria has made love to him three times that day. The relationship that exists between husband and wife is purely sexual. There is no love and affection for each other.

In 'Orbiting', Vic, Renata's lover leaves her in a matter of fact way. Renata herself narrates how it all happens:

> One Sunday morning in March he kissed me awake as usual. He'd brought in the *Times* from the porch and was reading it… He said 'I'm leaving babe. New Jersey doesn't do it for me anymore.' I said, 'Okay, so where're we going?'… Vic said, 'I didn't say we, babe.' So I asked, 'You mean it's over? Just like that?' And he said, 'Isn't that the best way? No fuss, no hang-ups' (Mukherjee, 1990:62).

This particular incident shows how tenuous the relationship is that exists between lovers, a love not based on real undersanding.

In 'Danny's Girls', we see Danny Sahib, a young Dogra boy from Simla who earns a lot from his lucrative marriage business in America. He arranges marriages between beautiful Indian girls and Indian boys settled in America. Danny is a real thriver who makes a good fortune by using whatever skills that sell in the new land.

Most of the stories delineate the struggle for survival of the immigrants in the U.S.A. The atmosphere in America is suffused with violence and murder. It is a world operated by middlemen, drug pushers, pimps and other underworld men who exploit people to make a living. The immigrants face tough competition which makes them resort to any method to survive in the new land. Doc Healy advises Jeb (in 'Loose Ends'): 'If you want to stay alive… just keep consuming and moving like a locust' (45). This locust image suggests very accurately how human beings are turned into locusts for sheer survival. Jeb has been a mercenary killer for Mr. Vee. 'She might have been fourteen, brassy-haired with wide black roots… I did what I was paid for, I eliminated the primary target and left no traces' (47).

After going through these stories the reader gets a feeling of disgust at the murky atmosphere that prevails in America—men and women pursuing sex very freely, the sense of artificiality seen everywhere, violence and murder in American cities. What is really disturbing to the sensibility of the Indian reader is the use of sexual material very abundantly. A woman having a sexual affair with a male partner who is already married is not viewed as adulterous at all. No doubt, America also provides plenty of freedom and unlimited opportunities for personal and social advancement. Immigrants coming from different parts of the world freely intermix with other people leading to a better understanding of other cultures and traditions, thus promoting a feeling of true cosmopolitanism. But unfortunately, the American freedom and the melting pot atmosphere have been carried to excess and this gets reflected in their personal behaviour. While immigrants can always use their freedom very positively and purposefully to advance their social and cultural interest, this requires individual will and determination and sustained effort to establish their sense of rootedness in the new land of their choice.

Bharati Mukherjee presents one aspect of American social life—the murky, violent side. It is difficult to accept the author's apparent view that American society espouses only violence and uninhibited social behaviour. Nor is it true that all immigrants to America completely give up their traditional values and behaviour. Reality is perhaps more complex than the picture Mukherjee paints.

Mukherjee's use of language is in conformity with her immigrant theme. 'It is bare, functional and unselfconsciously, unemotional' (Chandra 1991:217). All her characters speak typical American English. The writer is so familiar with the American landscape that the reader comes to know the names of places, drinks, universities, shopping malls. Her use of colloquialism and slang is also masterly which shows that she herself, like her immigrant characters, has been fully transformed in her new land. She resorts to both irony and satire to reveal the superficial aspects of American life and the hypocritical attitude along with the survival instinct of the American socio-cultural fabric. She also uses appropriate imagery to bring out the American social life surcharged with violence. Human beings are compared to locusts. 'Miami smells of the fecund rot of the jungle' (Mukherjee 1990:45). It is a dog-eat-dog kind of atmosphere that prevails in America. In spite of the brazen American flavour of English in Bharati Mukherjee's writings, one also comes across the occasional sprinkling of Indian words—like 'mangalasutra' which reminds readers of Indian traditions.

Mukherjee also uses Indian names for the protogonists of her stories—leaving us with the view that she has not completely forgotten Indian customs and habits. For immigrants, the move to America gives them enormous freedom and opportunity to pursue their goals contributing thereby to their personal and social advancement. As Hancok puts it (1987:303), 'the breaking away from rigidly predictable lives frees them to invent more satisfying pasts and gives them a chance to make their future in ways that they could not have in the Old World.... In immigrating... the characters become creators. By creating, they become real themselves, instead of unreal.'

Works Cited

Chandra, Subash. 1991. 'Americanness of the Immigrants in *The Middleman and Other Stories*.' R.K. Dhawan (ed). *Indian Women Novelists*. New Delhi: Prestige Books. 210–18.

Hancok, Geoff. 1987. *Canadian Writers at Work*. Toronto: Oxford University Press.

Inamdar, F.A. 1991. 'Immigrant Lives: Protagonists in Bharati Mukherjee's *The Tiger's Daughter* and *Wife*.' R.K. Dhawan (ed). *Indian Women Novelists*. New Delhi: Prestige Books.

Mukherjee, Bharati. 1990. *The Middleman and Other Stories*. New Delhi: Penguin.

Indian Englishes and the Indian Short Story in English

T. SRIRAMAN

An attempt is made in this paper to draw attention to the many kinds or layers of Indian English and to the fact that their existence has not been fully exploited by Indian fiction writers in English. I briefly discuss two short stories where such an attempt has been made. Towards the end I also attempt to see the reasons for the relative absence of varieties of Indian English in Indian fiction in English.

Why should creative writers in India choose the English language as their medium? This question (as well as the counter question, why not?) rightly strikes us today as unnecessary and anachronistic. It was however, a crucial question in the 1960s and 70s when Indian writing in English (till then called Indo-Anglian writing) was being established as a literature and as a field of study in its own right. We might remember Buddhadeva Bose's polemical 'entry' on 'Indian Poetry in English' in *The Concise Encyclopaedia of English and American Poets and Poetry* (1963) and also the questionnaire (based on Bose's entry) which P. Lal prepared and sent to a large number of Indian poets in English. The questionnaire and the replies sent by the poets were included in the volume edited by Lal, *Modern Indian Poetry in English: An Anthology and a Credo* (1969). It is not necessary now (especially when the term 'Indian Writing or Literature in English' would seem to have made way for 'Indian English Literature') to go into the details of the debate at that time. Suffice it to say that the basic issue was one of *authenticity*, the authenticity of the experience embodied in a language which, whatever else it was, was not the poet's mother tongue.

It is not known whether a similar questionnaire was ever sent to Indian fiction-writers in English. But novelists and critics did examine the issue, though the extent of the debate here was not as considerable as in the case of poetry. Raja Rao's famous 'Foreword' to *Kanthapura* (1937), Mulk Raj Anand's paper entitled 'The Changeling' (1972), Meenakshi Mukherjee's chapter 'The Problem of Style' in *The Twice Born Fiction* (1971) are some examples of such discussions.

The problem of authenticity, in the case of fiction writers, was two-fold: (a) they were writing in a language that was not their own, and (b) they were writing in English about people who do not normally speak or think in English. The first problem was not as important as the second because, if a writer was not at home in English, he or she would not attempt creative writing in English at all. The second problem was more real and serious but the general view was that the novelists had solved it by means of experiments in style. These experiments could be classified under three heads:

1. The introduction of words from the Indian languages through transliteration (e.g. *koi hai?*, *nahin, burra sahib*, etc.).
2. Experiments in diction and imagery through literal translation from the Indian languages (e.g. 'a rain of flowers', 'always the same Ramayana', 'may she have a hundred male issues', 'a rich whispering like a crowd at evening worship'—all from Raja Rao's *The Cow of the Barricades*).
3. Experiments in syntax (fashioning English syntax on the syntactic lines of Indian languages), e.g. 'He had one servant, two servants, and three servants' (Raja Rao, in *The Cow of the Barricades*).

The point to note about these linguistic features is that they were all part of these fiction writers' attempt to 'Indianise' English or in other words to evolve an Indian English to suit their purposes. They were mostly innovations by the writers themselves and not transcripts of actual Indian English speech or writing. Even if we do not accept the view that these innovations were assertions of identity on the part of the colonial or post-colonial subject, we must at any rate grant that they were techniques adopted by the writers for artistic purposes, to achieve authenticity either for the entire narration (as for example in the case of *Kanthapura*) or for individual characters (as in the case of Anand and many others). In any case, to repeat the point made earlier, such uses of Indian English do not necessarily reflect actual Indian English usage.

The stylistic divide I wish to consider in this paper is different from the ones discussed above. One definition of style could be that it is the exploitation of different existing varieties of the language in question. It follows then that the Indian creative writer has at his or her disposal the multiple layers or varieties of Indian English with all their social and cultural moorings and that these provide the writer the opportunity not only to individualise characters but more importantly, to delineate social class distinctions as well as the desire, fulfilled or frustrated, to achieve mobility. I venture to say that this particular linguistic fact—the existence of different layers or kinds of Indian English—has not been exploited in a significant way or to a considerable extent by Indian fiction writers in English. I shall illustrate the divide presently with the help of two short stories but before that I should perhaps make clear what I mean by the layers of Indian English.

One of the important changes that has come about in linguistic studies in the last few decades is 'the shift from language as a uniform and invariant structure to language in all its variety' (Parasher 1991:1). If Indian English is indeed a variety of English, it has within it many sub-varieties. These sub-varieties could be described, as the varieties of other languages have been described by socio-linguists, on the basis of regional, registral, and proficiency levels. While the question of a standard or model is by no means easy to answer—we should remember that there is as yet no dictionary or grammar of Indian English—the existence of a good number of sub-varieties has not been in doubt, though it must be admitted once again that except for its phonology, no other aspect of Indian English has been extensively or satisfactorily described (Parasher 1991:63). It is agreed that Indian English is not one but many, that there is a cline (if we take proficiency levels alone) ranging from the highly educated variety of Indian English (which indeed, in lexis and grammar if not in pronunciation, may be no different from educated British or American English) to the least educated variety which may include or stop short of code-mixing. It is also recognised now that these varieties (once again especially of proficiency levels) are often class-determining and status-determining and that the attainment of one level may indicate, if not bring about, movement from one class to another (or at least give one the illusion of doing so). In either case, such stratification and its socio-cultural implications hold interesting possibilities for the Indian fiction-writer in English.

The device I have in mind has been employed in poetry by Nissim Ezekiel in his 'Very Indian Poems in Indian English' to draw 'linguistically and culturally sensitive caricatures' (Perry 1992:245) of either lower middle class or upper class (as in 'Goodbye Party for Miss Pushpa T.S.'). We might have different views about the writer's attitude to the speakers in these poems—whether it is condescending or compassionate—but Ezekiel is clearly presenting classes of Indians. Such an attempt to define classes of Indians (and the relationships amongst them) in terms of the Englishes they use has not frequently been made in fiction.

Meenakshi Mukherjee in *The Twice Born Fiction* cites an example of a novel where language becomes an important issue. The novel is Manohar Malgonkar's *Combat of Shadows* (1963). Language here is thematic because it symbolises the social relations between the British in India and the Anglo-Indians. The relationship between Henry Winton, a pucca Englishman and a British public school product and Ruby Miranda, an Anglo-Indian girl from a railway colony, breaks down first because of their linguistic incompatibility (Ruby is always saying things like 'Ta muchly', 'Give's a fag' or 'He was sweet on me—my, he was really jay'). However, though her speech patterns get greatly refined in the course of the novel (like Eliza Doolittle's in *Pygmalion*), her ultimate Anglo-Indian dream (viz. to be admitted into European society through marriage) is shattered at the end since her race and class are still barriers (Mukherjee 1971: 188–89).

Why have not more fiction-writers attempted such socio-linguistic-cultural representations? Malgonkar in *Combat of Shadows* was writing about two classes of people for both of whom English (two different varieties of course) was the mother tongue. One thinks in this context not only of those British and American novels where dialects or other varieties are symbolic of social relationships (like *Lady Chatterley's Lover, The Catcher in the Rye* or Alan Sillitoe's long short story 'The Loneliness of the Long-Distance Runner') but also of early Caribbean novels like Naipaul's *A House for Mr. Biswas.* Meenakshi Mukherjee (1971:173) explains this lack as follows:

> The Indo-Anglian novelist has no such device at his disposal because although Indians speaking in English do have certain characteristic modes of expression, he is not necessarily writing about that very small minority who speak English all the time, nor about those few situations in which many Indians are forced to speak some variety of English. He is generally dealing with non-English speaking people in non-English speaking situations.

This was written in 1971 and the difference now is that even though the people who speak English all the time are still a minority—but we should remember that this minority now includes not only Anglo-Indians but a larger number of other Indians whose mother tongue is not English—'the situations in which many Indians are forced to speak some variety of English' are increasing in number as well as in socio-cultural importance.

Let us turn now to the two stories which led me to these observations.

Khushwant Singh's 'A Bride for the Sahib' (Singh 1989) (my first story) is different from the other stories (such as 'Karma' or 'Man, How the Government of India Run') in which he presents varieties of Indian English in that here the linguistic factor is crucial and thematic. Mr. Santosh Sen (his first name is changed to Sunny by the boys at the Anglo-Indian school, just as Upamanyu Chatterjee's hero has his very Indian name Agastya changed to the very English August), a Balliol product, whose inability to speak an Indian language was no handicap to his entering the Indian Administrative Service, has just got married at the Registry to a traditional Bengali girl (largely because his mother wanted to see him 'settled'). Sen is what the English contemptuously described as a wog—a westernised oriental gentleman. The story begins a few hours after the wedding (which he has tried to keep as quiet as possible, but it was 'impossible to keep anything a secret for too long in his nosey native land'), with his clerical subordinates at the office coming to greet him in the following way:

> 'Saar' began the superintendent of the clerical staff, 'Whee came to wheesh your good shelph long liphe and happinesh' (128).

He simply waves them back to their respective desks and asks the Superintendent to see him later about the redistribution of work when he is away (on honeymoon, though he does not tell them that). The Superintendent responds with 'Shuttenly, Saar'. Sen does inadvertently mention the proposed honeymoon to a Punjabi colleague Santa Singh, but when the Sardar proceeds to offer earthy advice on how to make the honeymoon successful, Sen interrupts and dismisses him with a handshake. And Sen is relieved that 'he had behaved with absolute rectitude—exactly like an English gentleman' (131).

As Sen drives back home for lunch he wonders whether his wife would be a Memsahib:

> Would his wife be a Memsahib, he mused as he drove back home for lunch. It was not very likely. She claimed to be an M.A. in English literature. But he had met so many of his countrymen with long strings of firsts who could barely speak the English language correctly. To start with, there was the Director himself with his 'okey dokes' and 'by gums' who, like other South Indians, pronounced eight as 'yate', an egg as a 'yagg' and who always stumbled on words beginning with an 'M'. He smiled to himself as he recalled the Director instructing his private secretary to get Mr. M.M. Amir, Member of Parliament, on the phone. 'I want Yum Yum Yumeer, Yumpee'. The Bengalis had their own execrable accent: they added an airy 'h' whenever they could after a 'b' or a 'w' or an 's'. A 'virgin' sounded like some exotic tropical plant, the 'vharjeen', 'will' 'wheel' and 'simple' as a 'shimple' (132–33).

The last-mentioned Bengali speech habit is to wreck Sen's marriage. As he and his bride Kalyani drive on their honeymoon trip Sen behaves like the perfect English gentleman towards his wife (who had drawn her sari over her forehead) asking her only questions like 'Does the smoke [from his pipe] bother you?' She only replies with vigorous shakes of the head. On arrival at the rest-house he goes out for a stroll, returns and sits in the verandah for a drink before dinner:

> It was no point asking his wife to sit with him. He poured himself a large Scotch and lit his pipe. Once more his thoughts turned to the strange course his life had taken. If he had married one of the English girls he had met in his university days how different things would have been. They would have kissed a hundred times between the wedding and the wedding night… The whisky warmed his blood and quickened his imagination. He was back in England. The gathering gloom and the dark, tropical forest accentuated the feeling of loneliness. He felt an utter stranger in his own country. He did not hear the bearer announcing that dinner had been served (135–36).

And it is at this moment that the linguistic tragedy (which is the prelude to the conjugal calamity) strikes. 'Now his wife came out and asked in her quaint Bengali accent…' (136).

Well, this is the first time she speaks to him and what she wants to ask is, 'Do you want to sit inside?' but she adds the inevitable Bengali 'h' to her 's'. 'What' he asks gruffly, waking up from his reverie. She repeats the question the same way, adding now, 'The deener ees on the table.' Sen is shocked:

> Good Lord! What would his English friends have said if she had invited them in this matter! The invitation to defecate was Mrs. Sen's first communication with her husband (136).

Neither Sen nor the marriage recovers from this shock. During dinner, he clears his throat many times to start a conversation but cannot think of anything to say. He is honest enough to think of what his friends might say:

> 'Oh Sunny Sen! How could he start talking to his wife? He hadn't been properly introduced. Don't you know he is an Englishman?' (136)

After dinner, as he goes into the bedroom to fetch his transistor radio set (to listen to the news) he notices that the beds have been laid side by side and that the sheets have been sprinkled with perfume 'as if they also awaited the consummation of the marriage performed earlier in the day':

> How, thought Sen, could she think of this sort of thing when they hadn't even been introduced! No, hell, barely a civil word had passed between them? (137)

And so, while Mrs. Sen collects her betel-leaf case and disappears into the bedroom, Sen sits on in the dining room most of the night listening to the news and later to a concert by the Czech Philharmonic now on a visit to India. The 'honeymoon' is brought to an end the next morning by an urgent official summons for Sen. Kalyani goes back to her parents' house. Sen first refuses to fetch her back but agrees, on the persuasion of his mother, to her being brought back by an uncle of his. The day she comes back, Sen returns home from office well after midnight after spending the evening at the Gymkhana club and having dinner at a friend's. There is no light in her bedroom. He retires to his own bedroom. The next morning the bearer wakes him up and says Memsahib hasn't got up yet and that her door is bolted from the inside. Master and servant then break into Memsahib's room and find her still, her eyes staring fixedly through the thick glasses.

> Sen put his hand on her forehead. It was the first time he had touched his wife. And she was dead (143).

But Mrs. Sen had died only after committing, ignorantly though, another grievous linguistic sin:

> On the table beside the bed was an empty tumbler and two envelopes. One bore her mother's name in Bengali: the other was for him. A haunted smile came on his lips as he read the English address:
>
> 'To,
> Mr. S. Sen, Esq.'
>
> (ibid.)

My other story for illustrating the exploitation of Indian Englishes is Shashi Tharoor's 'The Village Girl' (included in a collection of early stories called *The Five-Dollar Smile* 1990). Sundar, a young Delhi collegian, is on his annual visit to his native village in Kerala (made against his will at the insistence and in the company of his parents). As the father goes out catching up on old friends, the mother receives a visit from an old family friend called Narayani Amma who is accompanied by her niece. A reluctant Sundar is introduced to the shy seventeen-year old Susheela (who has just passed S.S.C. in the English medium), and she strikes him (in her sitting position) as a member of the species whom he and his Delhi friends would have called *behenjis*, 'an ironic reference to the fact that no one in his right mind would try to flirt with one':

> They wore floral-patterned *salwar-kameez* with nylon *dupattas* and scarlet polish was forever flaking off their nails. They also chattered on buses in Hindi or Punjabi and spoke English, if at all, in an accent you could have ground *dal* with. Here in Kerala, you had to allow for regional variations of dress and patois, but Sundar could spot a *behenji* at fifty paces, and though the word didn't exist locally in Malayalam, it was clear that a *behenji* was what she was (Tharoor 1990:43–44).

The aunt wants the niece to say something in English to the Delhi folk but the poor girl only simpers her embarrassment. To make matters worse, Sundar's mother insists on his taking the girl round their huge garden. But as they walk together she looks less like a *behenji* and more like a pretty girl 'in a typically Malayalee way.' When he shows her the garden—without being able to name any plant or flower there—she simply says 'It is beautiful' and Sundar 'could almost imagine her reciting the "Yinglish" sounds from a list of phonemes in Malayalam script.'

She addresses him as Sundar *etta* (elder brother) ('Ironic transference,' he thinks, 'the *behenji* had gone and made an elder brother out of him') and he says in some irritation, 'Forget about this *etta* business, Susheela. I'm only nineteen, for Christ's sake.' She can't understand—and she says so—the meaning of 'for Christ's sake', nor why he should say it when he is not a Christian. She wants to ask him a whole lot of questions:

> 'Sure,' he replied uneasily. This was going to be like no conversation he had ever had. Conversing as an *etta* to a

> village *behenji* in primary school English was going to be, he reflected, a whole new scene (49).

Now they are both seated on the smooth stone floor and Susheela continues her puzzled and excited inquiry:

> But it is all very strange to me. Like you're always saying 'Sorry' and 'Thank you' in English.
>
> 'What's wrong with saying sorry and thank you?' he asked, fishing for his cigarettes.
>
> 'Nothing, of course, but it's not Indian', she said. 'We are not having any word for "sorry" and "thank you" in Malayalam language. In our culture you are supposed to show your sorrow, or your gratefulness-gratitude, by your normal actions and expressions. This English way, it is as if one or two words are enough to pay your debt. Isn't it?'
>
> Sundar had found his pack. 'I guess I haven't thought about it that way,' he admitted, taking out a cigarette (50).

Susheela wants to know all about his life in Delhi; she herself has never left even the district:

> 'I can see you are so modern, Sundar *etta*. Here in the village I am knowing nothing of the kind of life you are leading in the big city. It must be so different. Please describe it to me, Sundar *etta*. I am really wanting to know' (52).

As he warms to the job and describes his world to her, she listens with rapt attention:

> Had he stepped out of a spaceship on Mars he could not have been greeted with more avid, and admiring curiosity. Each answer, each trivial detail, seemed to elevate him in her esteem; he was unique, her sole means of access to a world she knew existed with which she had no contact (52).

Soon he finds himself asking her about her plans. She would like to go to college but her father cannot and will not send her to college; in fact she is to be married soon to a drunkard widower with a child. Sundar is shocked at the injustice and callousness of it all. The girl breaks down at this stage and as Sundar touches her cheeks to wipe away her tears, he finds himself making love to her. It is all so unpremeditated and when it is over Sundar is filled with remorse.

> He had ruined her. He had destroyed the illusions of a simple village girl, a nervous, trusting young thing who called him Sundar *etta* (54).

As they walk back in the dark towards the house,

> … he caught her by the arm and, in a strangulated voice, spoke the only words that occurred to him: 'I'm sorry', he said.
>
> She had taken the first step from the yard to the porch and the moonlight suddenly bathed her face. It was lit up in the radiance of dreams fulfilled, and her smile was no longer that of a nervous girl, but of a woman who had touched a happiness she had not expected to be hers.
>
> A cloud passed, but Sundar found himself grateful for the darkness.
>
> 'Thank you,' she said, 'Thank you Sundar' (54–55).

Tharoor's story, though it does not represent his mature, much more sophisticated, later work, still explores, as does Khushwant Singh's story, social and cultural class relationships through juxtapositions of levels of Indian English. The movement, achieved or not, from one class to another is symbolised here by clear linguistic markers associated with one or the other class.

Perhaps we can now return to the questions why our fiction writers have made such infrequent or limited use of this linguistic device. The answer may have something to do not only with the status of English but with the attitudes and associations it evokes in the consciousness of the writer and the reader. In a chapter entitled 'Re-placing Language: Textual Strategies in Post-colonial Writing' in *The Empire Writes Back,* Bill Ashcroft and others mention two processes by which post-colonial writing defines itself (Ashcroft, et. al. 1989:38):

> The first, the abrogation or denial of the privilege of 'English' involves a rejection of the metropolitan power over the means of communication. The second, the appropriation and reconstitution of the language of the

> centre, the process of capturing and remoulding the language to new usages, marks a separation from the site of colonial privilege (Ibid.).

In the very early stages of Indian fiction in English, such abrogation and appropriation had clearly not taken place. There was an obvious anxiety to write 'correct, idiomatic' English which we find in early writers like Madhavaiah or K.S. Venkataramani—and this not only in their authorial narratives but also in the dialogues they assign to characters. This is ironic especially in Venkataramani's case in view of 'the aggressively nationalistic themes' of his works (Mukherjee 1971:193). The processes of abrogation and appropriation have clearly been accomplished in their novels by Raja Rao and Anand through devices like the use of 'untranslated words', 'syntactic fusion', 'code-switching and vernacular transcription', etc. (Ashcroft, et al. 1989:64, 68, 72). But the process at work in the stories we have discussed is rather different.

The authors of *The Empire Writes Back* speak of language variance in a post-colonial text as being 'profoundly metonymic of cultural difference' (53). The use of such language variance, especially the contrast between 'an appropriated English' and another 'still tied to the imperial centre' (59) captures the struggle between 'the culture affirmed on the one hand "indigenous" or "national" and that characterised on the other as "imperialist", "metropolitan", etc.' (53). The examples that are discussed, such as the passages from the play *The Cord* by the Malaysian writer K.S. Maniam and from a novel by the African writer Amos Tutuola all set up such a struggle, with the culture represented by English clearly challenging that symbolised by English.

What we have in our two short stories is of course a clear contrast between the English of the metropolitan centre—Sen, besides being a 'wog' is also a member of the ruling class and Sundar is a young man from the capital city with an English education—and the English of the periphery (clearly marked as 'regional' in the case of both Kalyani and Susheela in the two respective stories). But what is significant in both these cases is in a sense the continuing authority and fascination exercised by the former, viz. the metropolitan 'norm'. The 'Mr. S. Sen, Esq.'

written by Kalyani and the 'Thank you Sundar' spoken by Susheela are both a recognition of their submission to this norm. On the other hand, there is a 'struggle' indicated through the contrition felt by the male protagonists in both cases towards the end: Sen touches his wife for the first time and Sundar feels he has 'ruined' a 'simple village girl'. But their final response is ambivalent: the haunted smile that comes on Sen's lips as he reads the English address on the envelope could be one of derision mingled with guilt and compassion, and Sundar can only resort to the metropolitan 'I'm sorry', as though, as Susheela pointed out earlier, he can show his sorrow and be done with it in one or two words.

Clearly then, the acts of abrogation and appropriation are by no means total or complete. However the contrasts presented evidently reflect the psychological characterstics of a post-colonial society and the compulsions felt by the various social and cultural groups in relation to 'English' and 'english'.

The struggle in *The Great Indian Novel* (1989), Shashi Tharoor's later and more mature work, on the other hand, is between nationalist forces and the colonisers themselves; and the struggle is linguistic as well as political and social. At first sight, Tharoor seems to go a step further than the earlier Indian fiction-writers in English and throw the appropriated forms at the head of the colonisers themselves. Jayaprakash Drona, now a minister in Independent India, receives a petition from Ronald Heaslop (obviously a parody of E.M. Forster's character in *A Passage to India*), a British ICS Officer continuing in India Government service after Independence. The petition is for restitution for the losses Heaslop had suffered during the Partition riots. But Drona suddenly remembers that Ronald Heaslop had, in his days of colonial arrogance, humiliated him (Drona) and so Drona now decides to take revenge. The administrative revenge is on Heaslop but the linguistic revenge is on all British ICS officers. So with Heaslop sitting before him, Drona summons the Secretary, another Englishman, and deliberately speaks swadeshi English, or 'Indian English' as the erstwhile colonisers would have branded it contemptuously. He wants them to see that he now has 'both an axe and an accent to grind':

'Ah, Sir Bewerley,' Drona said expansively. 'You were

putting a certain file before me, isn't it? File of Shri Heaslop? You have it?'

The Secretary handed it over with a set face.

'Now, let me see.' Drona examined the paper before him with exaggerated care. 'What is it you are proposing, Sir Brewerley? "Special one-time grant in partial restitution for losses suffered to private property in performance of service-related functions." My, my, what long sentence, Sir Bewerlily. I must be learning how to write like this soon. Otherwise how I will manage when you and your fellow British are no longer remaining here?...' (241)

Drona turns down Heaslop's request and the Secretary's recommendation and suggests instead that the latter start a collection for Heaslop. As his own contribution, he pours a fistful of small coins into Heaslop's lap.

If Jayaprakash Drona had really done all this, it would have been the Empire almost literally writing back or talking back deliberately in english with a small e, and it would have constituted an undisguised rejection of English with the capital E. But Tharoor's narrator Ved Vyas (VV for short) ruefully tells his scribe Ganapathi (after the latter had taken down all this!) that this was all only his own vengeful imagination and it did not happen that way at all! In fact, says Ved Vyas, Drona not only approved the restitution but obligingly ordered a transfer for Heaslop away from his troublesome district to the Secretariat in Delhi.

It is not clear what we are to make of this volte-face. While VV's 'vengeful imagination' conjures up a speech-act clearly constituting both abrogation and appropriation, the 'actual happening' could well be ambivalent. The latter could symbolise continuing capitulation to the erstwhile imperial power; it could on the other hand, suggest an acceptance of Indian English or rather Indian Englishes among Indians, without anyone finding it necessary to refer it back to, or throw it back at, the British. VV does not tell us exactly in what variety of English Drona orders the transfer which Heaslop seeks. However, while Drona might not have spoken to Heaslop and Sir Beverley 'with an axe and an accent to grind', perhaps he would not have minded at all if one of his own Indian colleagues had spoken english (unlike

Khushwant Singh's Sunny Sen who would certainly have minded it)!

Works Cited

Anand, Mulk Raj. 1978. 'The Changeling.' Ramesh Mohan (ed). *Indian Writing in English.* Papers read at the Seminar on Indian English held at the Central Institute of English and Foreign Languages, Hyderabad, July 1972. Bombay: Orient Longman.

Ashcroft, Bill, Gareth Griffiths and Helen Tiffin. 1989. *The Empire Writes Back: Theory and Practice in Post-Colonial Literature.* London-New York: Routledge.

Bose, Buddhadeva. 1963. 'Indian Poetry in English.' Stephen Spender and Donald Hall (eds). *The Concise Encyclopaedia of English and American Poets and Poetry.* London: Hutchinson.

Ezekiel, Nissim. 1989. 'Very Indian Poems in Indian English.' *Collected Poems. 1952–1988.* Delhi: Oxford University Press.

Lal, P. (ed.). 1969. *Modern Indian Poetry in English: An Anthology and a Credo.* Calcutta: Writers' Workshop.

Malgonkar, Manohar. 1963. *Combat of Shadows.* London: Hamish Hamilton.

Mukherjee, Meenakshi. 1971. *The Twice Born Fiction.* New Delhi: Heinemann.

Parasher, S.V. 1991. *Indian English: Functions and Form.* New Delhi: Bahri Publications.

Perry, John Oliver. 1992. *Absent Authority: Issues in Contemporary Indian English Criticism.* New Delhi: Sterling.

Raja Rao. 1938. *Kanthapura.* London: George Allen & Unwin Ltd.

Singh, Khushwant. 1989. *The Collected Short Stories of Khushwant Singh.* Delhi: Ravi Dayal Publisher.

Tharoor, Shashi. 1989. *The Great Indian Novel.* New Delhi: Penguin Books.

—. 1990. *The Five-Dollar Smile: Fourteen Early Stories and a Farce in Two Acts.* New Delhi: Viking.

Language Dialectic and Fakir Mohan's Rhetoric of Progress

SACHIDANANDA MOHANTY

The social realism of the early Oriya novelist Fakir Mohan Senapati is marked, among other things, by the debate over the English language and its selective appropriation by the emerging bourgeoisie in the colonial State. The response to the English language and western education in Fakir Mohan is often seen as complex and problematic. There is of course a clear disavowal of neat polarisations such as Tradition—Modernity, Orality—Literacy, the English language—the vernacular. However, while education is strongly upheld as a major objective, westernisation, primarily seen as propelled through the English language is often equated with the 'colonising' agenda of the colonial State.[1]

Focussing on Fakir Mohan's memorably poignant tale 'Dakamunshi'[2] ('The Postman') this essay elucidates Fakir Mohan's attitude towards the introduction of the English language and the preservation of indigenous knowledge systems in the late nineteenth century. Social villains, morally renegade and ethically reprehensible are often shown, as in 'Dakamunshi', using the English languae. At such times, the English language becomes both threatening and menacing, upsetting the virtues of the traditional social order. Its secular, scientific and modernising role underlined by many colonisers is seen here as entailing a violation of the private and public ethic, thereby critiquing the notion of progress.

The opening of 'Dakamunshi' offers, through a series of compressed statements, a design that carefully conflates the ideological with the fictional. The opening sentence makes a prefatory reference to the protagonist Hari Singh, the Postman's numerous anonymous postings in the districts. In contrast, only his latest assignment is somehow found worthy of mention: Cuttack Sadar or Cuttack city. There is a rationale here. The privileging of Cuttack city as the centre of political and administrative power appears to be obvious. Hari Singh's years of devoted service have led to his promotion as the Head Peon. He has, one might say, finally arrived! But his sense of joy is actually a source of mixed blessings. For, not even nine royal rupees are enough when one has to buy a matchstick to light a fire! At least four rupees must be sent home every month for the upkeep of his wife and son. In contrast to the wife who remains unnamed as a mark of her subservient status and role in the unfolding drama, the son bears the proud name of Gopal, or Krishna the saviour. The irony of the name is of course not lost upon the reader by the end of the tale.

Gopal is, of course, a very special boy. Unlike the many details of the father's day-to-day living which do not seem to merit any mention in the narrative, Gopal's life and activities are the object of meticulous interest. We are told for instance, that Gopal reads in the Upper Primary School. His monthly fees are two annas. And one has to shell out more as a matter of routine for slate, paper and books. The extra expense forces the old man to go without food at times. But he is not deterred, remaining firm in his resolution: 'If necessary I must starve but let Gopal read!'

Thus, the first paragraph introduces all the three characters. It situates the tale in Cuttack city that brings hope to Hari Singh of a rise in professional standing, status and material well-being through the primary agency of his son's education. The father's hard-earned money and the struggle he willingly embraces are seen here as a necessary trade-off for the rise of the son in the world, a supposedly 'normal' and commonplace motivation in a typically agrarian social order.

In the life of Hari Singh, a life that was barely manageable, there is now the unfortunate intervention of a crisis, introduced in the very first sentence of the second paragraph. Significantly, Hari Singh does not discover, by himself, the fact of his superannuation at the age of fifty-five. It is the Postmaster, who like Chitragupta, the heavenly Record Keeper, looks at the

'Service Book' of the old man and passes a solemn death sentence: 'Hari Singh, now you are fifty-five! Time for your pension! It's the end of your career!' Hari Singh's real worry is: 'What would happen to Gopal's education?' For, ever since Gopal's birth, it was the constant thought of Singh senior, that one day Gopal would become a Sub-Post Master, or at any rate, the village Post Master.

It is at this point in the tale that Fakir Mohan lets in the crucial operative detail: 'It's hard to get a good job unless one knows *English*!' Since there was no facility in the village, one had to bring Gopal to Cuttack in order to teach him English! Naturally, Singh loses considerable sleep over this issue. To Hari Singh, his boss the Post Master Babu appears to be God incarnate. He must constantly try and please him by running errands even outside his working hours. Hari Singh of course intuitively knows the cause of the Babu's supremacy. For the clue to the mystery is simply that the Post Master Babu is capable of reading *English* newspapers. As the narrator remarks: 'In the evening when the Babu relaxes in the armchair and reads the *English newspapers*, the "chillum" that Singh fixes, none can ever match him!' (emphasis mine).

Singh looks after the physical and medical needs of most authorities—from the Postal Inspector to the Superintendent who come to visit his post office. With superiors who are indulgent, it is not surprising that his plea for an extension in service is granted by his office. However, the calamity is far from over. A wire from home informs him that his wife is dying of a terminal illness. Singh reaches home in time to see the old woman 'touch the feet of her husband, fold her hands and close her eyes.' As the narrator observes with a note of dramatic foreshadowing: 'Everything was over! The *real household* of Singh was destroyed! He sold the few remnants of his possessions and came away to Cuttack with the child' (emphasis mine).

Thus, Singh's effort to provide English education to his son is partly aided by Providence as well. For he is able to bring his son to the city. The narrator continues recording the tribulations that the father braves when he has to manage with a meagre pension. Household vessels are sold and even the paltry amount in the Savings Bank is soon exhausted. Finally, the long cherished desire of the father is fulfilled. Gopal passes the examination and is appointed as the Sub-Post Master of Makrampur Post Office, thanks primarily to the influence of the Post Master Babu, his earlier benefactor.

Hari Singh's crowning glory contains the seeds of his defeat. The gratification of the unlettered father is equally matched by the increase in Gopal's overbearing arrogance and supercilious snobbery, his penchant for westernisation and above all, his fascination with the English language as a passport to enter the charmed inner circle of power. Hari Singh's singular effort has been to make a perfect 'Babu' out of his son. He must now rush to the market in search of suitable attire, shoes, trousers and coat. For his part, the son prefers to be known by the more honorific Gopal Chandra Singh rather than his former commonplace name 'Gopal' with its rather rustic connotations. The father observes with pride and satisfaction that Gopal sits in the office with five other colleagues and 'writes in English'. The reiteration of the primacy given to the English language throughout the tale underlines its increasing appropriation by the rising middle class for their own ends. Gopal is the perfect embodiment of his father's dream to be a Brown Sahib who can handle the English language. Gopal's contempt for his father can therefore only be a logical extension of his desire. As the narrator carefully observes:

> Now Gopal Babu's attitude has somewhat changed. These days, the very sight of his father provokes him. This one is a fool, an imbecile. *He does not know English*, wears dirty clothes. What will people say if you were to call him your father! Just the other day some educated women happened to come home. Imagine the cheek of the old man! Bare bodied he went past them! What shame! There would be no dignity left unless one forthwith removed him from sight! (emphasis mine).

Fakir Mohan's ideological interest in the English language's primary role in structures of power does not allow for any distraction in the narrative. The story rapidly moves in the direction of an inevitable tragedy as Singh's fate plummets. He is first prohibited from showing up before Gopal's friends and later, on a day of inspection, he is asked to carry the luggage of

'Gopal Babu' to the village. Fakir Mohan's narration of this turn of events is both tragic and poignant:

> The Babu got dressed. Shoving the umbrella into his armpit and circling his walking stick merrily, he went away. What could the old man do? Gathering everything, he made it into a bundle. He had no strength, nor could he walk. His eyes watered frequently. Every other step, he had to sit down. Towards evening, he arrived at Makrampur. Even as the old man paused to breathe, the Babu fired him for his delay.

As the old man's health rapidly deteriorates, Fakir Mohan offers the climaxing scene. The incessant coughing of the invalid disturbs the sleep of the son. Annoyed, he orders the peon to remove the old man sitting by the thorny fence outside. The reaction of the peon, as seen through the eyes of the narrator is noteworthy. As Fakir Mohan records:

> The peon of course is an illiterate. *He has not read English.* He has a native mind and heart. 'How could I possibly discard', he thought, 'the old invalid at the fence?' (emphasis mine)

If the peon represents grace and compassion, the traditional virtue of the dispossessed, then Gopal Babu's arrogant 'English' air has an insistent echo: 'Furious he gave two *English* blows to the old man and threw his bedding outside!' (emphasis mine).

In depicting this conflict between the opposing forces, Fakir Mohan does not lead the story to an unmitigated tragedy. Hari Singh's plight, bad enough, is arrested. The tale ends in a parting of ways between the father and son. The old man returns to his village and puts his modest property to share-cultivation. 'These days,' the narrator tells us, 'he sits on the verandah of his house and chants the name of God.'

It would be seen that in this delicate tale of filial relationships and changing values, Fakir Mohan is not offering us an ahistorical account of the plight of the individual vis-a-vis the insuperable forces of life, a kind of latter day Orestean tragedy. In 'Dakamunshi', Fakir Mohan's concern is more specific. Through the compelling tale, the author seems to be offering an ambiguous if not an unsympathetic account of English education in a feudal set up. While Fakir Mohan's pronounced interest in education as the primary means for emancipation and social mobility is well known,[3] he was equally sensitive to the way the rising middle class elite manipulated and appropriated modes of domination such as the alien language for exercising hegemony in a feudal, agrarian society. The learning of the language of the court such as Persian, Arabic, Urdu, and in this instance, English, has always entailed for the subjects, the enjoyment of political and administrative favours. In mid- and late nineteenth century British India, the creation of an intermediate class of beings, Macaulay's 'Indian by blood and English in temperament' as a buffer between the masters and the commoners, was inevitably part of the colonial agenda. As depicted by Fakir Mohan in 'Dakamunshi', the compulsion of social forces left little space for the middle class between the English language and the vernacular. The growing drive for the English language at the expense of the vernacular,[4] an unqualified espousal of westernisation and the western notion of progress at the expense of the indigenous knowledge systems, could only be the logical corollaries of this desire. In the course of the story the graded reiteration of the word, the term 'English' not only denotes the language as distinct from the vernacular, not only refers to the new western or English education, but also acquires connotations of an alien and arrogant set of attitudes and values. It speaks of the sharpness of Fakir Mohan Senapati's ideological vision that through his incisive social realistic narratives such as 'Dakamunshi' he offered a critique of the discourse of power based on language dialectics.

Notes

1. For further elaboration of the idea see Sachidananda Mohanty 1994.
2. Extracts quoted in the text are my translations from Senapati 1991.
3. The demand for jobs by Oriyas was acutely felt. As Fakir Mohan himself remarks in his poem 'Utkala Brahmana':

    All are foreigners—the babus and lawyers. Even the post office clerk is not one of us. (My translation.)

4. See Prafulla Chandra Mohanty 1985. As is well known, following Edward Said and others in the West, considerable work has been done in this regard by contemporary cultural critics such as Gauri Viswanathan, Rajeshwari Sunder Rajan, Kumkum Sangari, Svati Joshi. See for instance, Partha Chatterjee 1986, Gauri Viswanathan 1990, and many Subalterns who have followed the lead of scholars like Ranajit Guha, Partha Chatterjee and Sumit Sarkar.

Works Cited

Chatterjee, Partha. 1986. *Nationalist Thought and the Colonial World: A Derivative Discourse*. London: Zed Books.

Mohanty, Sachidananda. 1994. 'Rebati and the Woman's Question.' Paper presented at the National Seminar on Fakir Mohan Senapati, Department of Modern Indian Languages, Delhi University, March 1994.

Mohanty, Prafulla C. 1985. *The Picture of Contemporary Orissa in Fakir Mohan's Literature*. Cuttack: Friends Publishers.

Senapati, Fakir Mohan. 1991. *The Stories of Fakir Mohan Senapati*. Cuttack: Prachi Prakashan.

Viswanathan, Gauri. 1990. *Masks of Conquest: Literary Study and British Rule in India*. London: Faber and Faber.

English in the Telugu Short Story: Some Observations

M. KESHAV

The overarching aim of this paper is to show the impact of English literary tradition and language on modern Telugu short stories. But the thrust of this paper is to examine the use of English words and phrases in some stories of Buchi Babu and Kutumba Rao. The varied reasons for such a use of English words and phrases in their stories, are among other reasons, to make a character/situation authentic, or to achieve comic and satirical effects. I will examine the stories in order to show how these purposes manifest themselves by the presence of English words and phrases.

Before I go on to examine these aspects it is desirable to look at the impact of English literary tradition on the modern Telugu story. Telugu language and literature have, in general, been much influenced by various other foreign languages, particularly English. Story writing is not an exception to this influence. Story writing in Telugu as a form of creative expression is not a new phenomenon. The impact of the West which was mainly due to the introduction of English education in India, has, undoubtedly, been the main source of the new spirit of experimentation. The writer today is not blind to his own surroundings and the various transforming social forces in operation.

K. Veerabhadra Rao in his pioneering work *Telugu Sahityamu Pai English Prabhavam* (1986) attempts to study the impact of the West in general and of the British in particular on the life and letters of the Telugu people with special emphasis on the influence of English literature on Telugu literature. He says:

> Telugu literature has through the ages been influenced by a variety of literatures, foreign as well as Indian, and is none the worse for it. They enriched its vocabulary and enlivened its thought. In the past the influence was restricted to the languages of India and some languages of the Middle East, and with the impact of the West on India, the literatures of the West and chiefly English among them, exerted their influence on the form and content of Telugu literature... (translation mine).

He traces the entire history from the advent of European trading companies. He says that the British Raj not only established political institutions but also set up institutions to disseminate English education in India. As a result, he says a considerable number of English words/phrases found entry into Telugu writings. Some of them are 'company', 'soldiers', 'line', 'fire', 'officers', 'commandant', 'captain', 'colonel', 'Mr. Collector', 'English', 'pistol', 'counsel', 'receipt', etc. However some of these words/phrases were not directly transcribed into Telugu but with slight variations all of them are used in more than one place. For example, the word 'company' was used as 'kumpeny', 'line' as 'layanu', 'English' as 'Ingileezu'. Unfortunately he does not say much about the impact of English literary tradition on Telugu short stories, though he is of the opinion that some of the earlier writers clearly reflected the influence of English.

Another scholar who worked in this direction is Poranki Dakshinamurthy. In his outstanding work *Kathanika* (The Story) (1988), he traces the evolution of the Telugu short story from its origins to the present form. He extends his argument saying that all the changes that have taken place in the literary traditions of Russia, France and U.K. have inevitably come to Telugu stories also. And he is right in saying so because the changes occurring in the literary style of Telugu short stories approximate to similar changes occurring in other literatures. So in fact, the modern Telugu story is highly indebted to the English tradition for what it is today in the international context.

There are many writers who have been brought under the influence of English either directly or indirectly. The pioneer among such writers is Veeresalingam Panthulu whose novel *Rajasekhara Charitram* (1880) was based on Goldsmith's *The Vicar of Wakefield*. As part of a social and literary revolution Veeresalingam Panthulu ran a magazine titled *Vivekavardhani*. Veeresalingam Panthulu's statement from his magazine is quoted in Veerabhadra Rao (1986):

> ...it is admitted by one and all that western lore has worked wonders among the natives of India. We are quite aware that English education has rendered natives more refined in their manners, has dispelled the mist of superstition from the minds of several of them, if not many, and has considerably developed their moral calibre whenever it is properly imparted... (translation mine).

It is appropriate to mention that Veeresalingam Panthulu has even translated some of Charles Lamb's *Tales from Shakespeare* into Telugu. As an example I will mention the titles of a few of Veeresalingam Panthulu's stories which are actual translations from Shakespeare's own titles: *The Comedy of Errors* as 'Chamatkara Ratnavali'; *The Merchant of Venice* as 'Kurungeswara Vartaka Charitramu'; *The Taming of the Shrew* as 'Gayyalini Sadhucheyuta' and so on.

There was yet another pioneering attempt made by G. Apparao to revolutionise literature and language in Telugu. His early short stories especially 'Diddubattu', and 'Mee Peremiti...' have the traces of 'maturity' in writing that English literature is generally known for. Gurajada Apparao (as quoted in Veerabhadra Rao 1986) while acknowledging the influence of English, says 'the English do not subscribe to blind materialism, nor do they stray away from untruths. This I have learnt from studying their works' (translation mine). Since then the use of English words and phrases, at times direct translations of English sentences and ideas found their way into Telugu short stories.

II

I propose to first examine Buchi Babu's much cited and often discussed short story 'Chaitanya Sravanti' (1957). The title itself means 'the stream of consciousness'. One can easily see how Buchi Babu has been influenced by writers like James Joyce and Virginia Woolf who propounded and practised this narrative technique in their works. Buchi Babu himself says that he is deeply indebted to James Joyce for he was highly influenced by Joyce's *Ulysses* (1922). In fact, the story 'Chaitanya Sravanti' is a clear imitation of *Ulysses*. The story runs through a few hours of time, recording even the minute workings of the mind of the character. The hero in the story is a young, university graduate. He gets into a city bus to go for an interview. Before he gets off the bus, several things and ideas occur in his mind. All that happens in his mind and his reactions to the people he sees around and the different incidents that occur before his eyes evoke certain ideas and feelings in him. All this is recorded precisely in the story.

While doing so Buchi Babu uses about eighty English words such as 'film star', 'frequency', 'dismiss', 'repair', 'inflation', etc.; about twenty English phrases such as 'abstract art', 'gold medal', 'get out', 'basic values', etc. and about twenty references to English writers and their works such as Agatha Christie, Huxley, Hemingway, Keats, Milton, Whitman, Tolstoy, T.S. Eliot, D.H. Lawrence, etc.

These are the figures that the character thinks about while he is travelling. Now the question is, why does the author use such innumerable English words, phrases and ideas? One reason could be to elicit a proper response to his surroundings. Another reason is to make this character and his situation very authentic. Perhaps, it is an attempt to capture the stream of emotions, thoughts—disassociated and disjointed, yet occurring simultaneously in his mind. To do this very authentically, the writer cannot but capture the language of the mind. Then what is the language of such a literate person? Can one restrict oneself to the use of either only Telugu or only English while thinking?

III

There is yet another dimension to such a use of English words and phrases in Telugu short stories. This is to create a suitable environment in which characters speak. For this purpose, I intend to examine Kutumba Rao's story 'Tutor' (1968). This is one story where we find more than half of the sentences in English. Here the author does not even bother to translate the words and sentences into Telugu. Why does he do that? It is done for two important reasons. One is for creating a social environment, and the other is for comic and satirical effects.

Vani, the student in the story belongs to an upper middle class family. Her habits, language etc., are highly artificial, and excessively modern. To create such an environment from where she cannot see the other side of life, the author puts certain words, phrases and sentences into her mouth. She uses terms such as 'Femina', 'dear', 'fun', 'Digest', 'Sound of Music', 'Hatari', 'My Fair Lady', 'Cleopatra', 'deadly bore', 'Duty's duty', 'cheerio', 'plenty of money', and 'I am so sorry, teacher', etc. Most of these usages indicate her fun-loving nature and her complacent attitude to life. Using English words and sentences is a fashion for her. It shows her social status.

The other reason why the author uses such words and phrases is to mock at Vani and her life-style, thereby showing how empty and artificial she is. For example, every time Vani makes an attempt to impress the tutor by referring to 'money', 'charity', 'I am so sorry, teacher' (repeatedly used), 'plenty of money', 'plenty of fame', 'variety programme', etc., the author may be said to caricature a particular snobbish type of girl in this character. She becomes an object of comedy in the story rather than of seriousness by her attempts to impress others. In contrast, Rajasekhar, the tutor, who is already established and hard-working, does not find it necessary to impress. That is why we find limited use of English words and phrases in his speech.

IV

There are other inevitable reasons for such a use of English words in Telugu short stories. These inevitable reasons are of two kinds. One is when there are no alternative words. What alternatives can one find in Telugu for words like 'conductor', 'bus', 'probation', 'calender', 'bank', 'interview' (all of these are used in Buchi Babu's 'Chaitanya Sravanti')? The use of such terms in short stories proceeds from the fact that there are no Telugu equivalents. The other reason why the writer resorts to the use of English terms is for better and proper communication. The terms like 'polish', 'logic', 'excuse me', 'medical college', 'first class', 'wrong side', 'cash' (all these are used again in Buchi Babu's 'Chaitanya Sravanti') can convey the meaning the author wants in a better way, than their equivalent Telugu words which are not in general use by readers.

Works Cited

Buchi Babu. 1957. 'Chaitanya Sravanti'. Hyderabad: Adarsa Sahityamala.

Dakshinamurthy, Poranki. 1988. *Kathanika: Svarupa Svabhaavaalu*. Secunderabad: Shivaji Press.

Ramalingam, D. (ed.). 1988. *Telugu Katha*. New Delhi: Sahitya Akademi.

Veerabhadra Rao, Kothapalli. 1986. *Telugu Sahitayamu Pai English Prabhavam. (The Influence of English on Telugu Literature*). Secunderabad: Shivaji Press.

Viswanatha Reddy, Kethu. (ed.). 1988. *Kutumbarao Sahityam*. Vol. 2. Hyderabad: Visalandhra Publishers.

Problems in Translating 'Sati Savitri'

M. SRIDHAR AND ALLADI UMA

The activity of translation involves a set of possibilities and translators inevitably have to make a choice at any given time. This paper focusses on some practical problems we encountered while translating Peddibhotla Subbaramaiah's Telugu short story 'Sati Savitri' (1990) into English. Our observations on this translation can apply to other genres also.

At the beginning of the short story, there is a description of the sky from Rajani's window. We had translated it thus:

> Rajani stood by the window. All she could see of the limitless sky was only a portion, small, like a piece of paper. The sky was black and starless.

But in the final published version, it appears as:

> Rajani stood by the window. All she could see of the limitless sky was a portion, like a *shred* of paper. The sky was black and starless (our emphasis).

Although the connection between the first two sentences is evident, we feel now that it could have been made more explicit by adding 'from there' (as done by the author himself in the original) after 'limitless sky' to our first version or by combining the two sentences (taking some liberty to move slightly away from the original), a possibility which we did consider initially. Any of these choices does not seem to make a big difference when these lines are taken in isolation. However, 'the limitless sky' looking 'small, like a piece of paper' serves to reinforce Rajani's isolated predicament. Therefore, the choice of combining the two sentences or adding 'from there' brings the intended effect. Between these two possibilities, using the two sentences with the 'from there' connection looks more appropriate, as it takes us closer to the original. It is here that our understanding of the whole story plays a major role in the translation of the individual parts. In any case, the use of 'like a shred of paper'—unlike 'small, like a piece of paper'—suggests a life torn asunder. It is true that Rajani's life is disrupted because of her husband's death, loss of job, etc. But she has been depicted as having remained a part of society. Even physically speaking, for any person looking through a window only a portion of the sky would be visible. Rajani too looks upon her life as limited, albeit due to circumstances. Hence, our use of the earlier phrase 'small, like a piece of paper'. Here is an instance of translation involving the inevitable activity of interpretation.

Yet another occasion of our decision to deviate from the original is with regard to idiomatic and culturally-loaded expressions which are not easily translatable. For instance, the scene in the prison where Rajani's child's continuous crying disturbs the sleep of the other inmates and of the policeman keeping watch over them. All of them express their annoyance at Savitri's unwillingness to feed the baby. At this point the policeman remarks: 'ayina yeem pooyeekaalam vaccipadindiraa deevuda!' (322)

We translated this idiomatic expression as: 'What a terrible thing to happen!'

We did this to bring out the layers of meaning we feel the author is trying to convey—the nuisance caused by the child's crying and the terrible plight of the child not being fed by the (supposed) mother. By doing this we have, of course, entered the realm of interpretation again. If translated literally, it would have been: 'Oh God, even so what bad times have befallen us!'

This sounded clumsy to us. Instead, we could have used an expression like: 'What a nuisance!'

But this would have limited the possibilities of meaning to only one, that is, the nuisance caused to the people around. We therefore used the alternative expression 'What a terrible thing to happen!' This, like the author's own expression in Telugu, suggests the two readings but does not explicitly state either of them.

One more instance in the story reiterates our view of how an idiomatic expression in one language does not lend itself to easy translation into another. This is the scene where the policeman stops the rickshaw and interrogates the man with Savitri. The policeman's question when translated literally would read: 'What fate has befallen you that you take hold of this woman who sells her body and call her your wife?'

As we felt expressions such as 'kharma yeem pattindandii' and 'aadadanni pattukoni' (319) are not easily translatable, and when translated sound awkward, we translated the sentence as: 'Why do you have to call a prostitute your wife?'

However, we now feel that we could have used 'the woman who sells her body' instead of the term 'prostitute.'

We were confronted with a major problem when we thought about the title 'Sati Savitri'. With all its mythological and cultural connotations, what were we going to do about it—retain it, translate it or give a footnote in explanation? Of course, we retained it, especially in view of the fact that our translation was being published in *The Hindu* whose readers would need no explanation of either of the terms—Sati or Savitri. But what would we have done if the audience had been non-Indian? As argued earlier in the paper, translating a culturally-loaded expression like this seemed cumbersome. But by not translating it, we would have prevented non-Indian readers from understanding some other dimension of the story. For instance, the name of Savitri, who is a representation of a virtuous wife, is here the name of a prostitute. Then, the application of multiple levels of meaning associated with the term 'Sati'. The other choice would have meant giving a long explanatory note by which we as translators would have stepped into the role of editors. Would it then have been better to leave the whole title in italics and make the readers, whoever they may be, look up the terms, as we do so often, when confronted with foreign myths and expressions? To us the last choice seemed to be the best.

There were occasions when we had to make a departure from the original expression. For instance, there is a description of darkness by the author at the beginning of the story: 'pilistee badulu palukutundeemoo annanta dattangaa cikkagaaundi ciikati.'

When translated literally this sentence would read something like this: 'The darkness is so densely packed as if it would respond if called out to.'

To us, a description like this in English looked rather awkward. Therefore, we took the liberty of bringing out the core of this description by translating it into a cryptic expression, 'impenetrable darkness'. It is true that the implicit metaphor of a densely packed darkness is lost in this option. Between sounding awkward while retaining the original description, and capturing the tenor of the description, we exercised the latter choice.

Expression in English in the process of translation constitutes more than choosing appropriate words. It involves decision-making at another important level—that of indication of time, especially when the original text is in a language like Telugu. For example, the sentence with which the story begins— 'Rajani kitikii daggariki vacci nilabadindi' (315)—can be taken to be either in the present or the past and can be translated as: 'Rajani stands by the window' or 'Rajani stood by the window.' As the Telugu text employed time in this ambiguous fashion, we were faced with the problem as to what time markers to use in our English translation. We had originally used the present tense throughout the story. However, at the suggestion of the editor we changed it to the past tense. Reflecting on it, we still feel the story would have been more effective if it were in the present tense as it would have brought out the immediacy of the story. Also, we find the writer having used the present continuous marker at certain places as in: 'varsham chappudu ceestuu kurustunnadi' (317)—'The rain is falling continuously, noisily'. Sentences like this in the present continuous confirm our view that we should have used only the present tense. However, we recognise the question of the choice of time markers as a perpetual problem for which there are no ready solutions. Each case must be examined independently and a decision taken considering its appropriateness in the given situation.

Insights into the differences in the nature of time markers in

Telugu and English gained through the process of translation could serve a pedagogical purpose in the teaching of English, especially to Telugu-English learners.

Work Cited

Subbaramaiah, Peddibhotla. 1990. *Peddibhotla Subbaramaiah Kathalu*. Hyderabad: Visalandhra Publishing House.

English and the 'Country' Short Story in India: A Responsibility

SUDHAKAR MARATHE

There is a situation developing in India to which no one really pays attention. In the march of what is called 'progress'—whether it is viewed with approbation or disaffection—rural India is taking a beating. Its face is changing at a rate difficult to imagine, aspects of its life are either already extinct or they are endangered. From my contact with environmental conservation I know, as some of you also may, that certain categories of concern have been created to define and to refer to similar phenomena. For instance, there is a world-wide list of endangered species; another list of plants and creatures which appear to be next in line may be found in the Red Data Book. Concern about these is reflected even in local organisations and societies. Further, much of this is indigenous effort. But no such specific concern seems to exist regarding 'indicators' of vanishing human phenomena around us.

Meantime, the people of the countryside are changing, their traditional professions and habitats and architecture and crafts are all disappearing into oblivion. Rope-making is now largely replaced by factory-made cordage; coppersmithy and brass works are now made obsolete by plastic and aluminium vessel factories; gathering of medicines and herbs, etc., are increasingly butted out of the way by the patent medicine industry; traditional costumes are disappearing, they are replaced by factory-made clothing of urban-western styles; ditto jewellery and decorations, and so on, specific to each community and sub-community and sub-region; traditional tools and processes are also disappearing. No voices seem to be raised against this human environmental degradation, no societies have been created for the conservation of these features of the ethos.

I would like to register here the idea that I am not in any way objecting to 'progress' for rural India. That is writing on the wall; it will come, and rural India as it was known until recently will vanish, needless to say in the process wiping out many horrors of country life which were especially the lot of the lower strata of country society—and that at least is a welcome side effect. Suffice it to say that rural people themselves may on occasion object to the progress or development models that are forced upon them. Witness the poetry of Bhujang Meshram, a tribal poet of Maharashtra, which tells us how, in this process which is called 'sanskritisation' in the abstract, his tribe can now be encountered *only* in a museum in the city!

Here are a couple of tentative translations by me from Meshram's volume of poems entitled *Ulgulan* (1990) (i.e., all-over simultaneous revolt)—

Jangad

Having entered their Dharmapeetha
First said,
'We're of the Yadav dynasty'

Second said,
'We, settled wanderers'

Third moaned,
'So what if we're Dhalias?'

Fourth laughed,
'We're Lambadas from the Dark'

Having heard all this out, unmoved,
'So how come you're still Jangad?'

So they all began looking to each other;
Then they saw only skeletons from Hadappa.

In search of an answer they entered the museum

It is said, they haven't come back yet....

And, this from 'Birsa Munda' from the same source—

True, you could say we're impatient
But we say 'Nay' to Sanskruti
Egzacly like our 'Nay' to Darkness....

My argument relates to a literary responsibility—if ever there was such a thing—for the English-educated people in India regarding this endangered way of life of some 70 per cent of our population, of the people who live outside 'city' and 'town', in the 'country'. By a predictable historical calculation, modern literature in India is considered to have been produced by city and town, with very occasional, usually condescending glances at the country. Such compositions as the country itself produced did not, first, reach the literate population, and, second, they were hardly even recorded (though now there are some people engaged in compilation of such records). In the literary sense, the Indian countryside was very nearly in limbo, despite its own abundant creativity, during the decades leading to our independence. And 'progress' in the decades following has not only ensured that everyone's gaze will be directed to the city and outward from there, but it has also rung the death-knell of the major part of the way of life which I indicate by the term 'country'. Incidentally, anyone is welcome to propose a term to apply to this entire way of life that is non-urban. But the terms 'rural' or 'grameen' tend to exclude non-agrarian people, locales, habitats, occupations and identities. At this point in my paper, therefore, I shall shift to the term 'country' to refer to both agrarian and non-agrarian, village or grameen as well as forest-dwelling (and even itinerant) ways of life, which have all already suffered considerable changes and will continue to do so until an unknown level of urbanisation has been attained across the country.

The responsibility to which I referred earlier concerns a record of these matters, both pre-modern ways of life and their confrontation with modernity. Whether the social sciences are doing enough in their own way to record country life in India is a moot question. Moreover, in general, social science records are dry, even when accurate. Only the arts, whether engendered in the countryside, or as a second best bet in the work of urban(ised) artists, could provide a feeling, an affectively human record, of events, relationships, objects and processes that are essentially country matters. Here, incidentally, is one reason why the short story may be of greater significance than the novel in our present context—writing a novel presumes a great depth of experience as well as sustained acts of writing. By its own constraints, the short story demands less general experience and less sustained or extended specificity of reference, since one location, one set of characters, one incident with a limited setting may do for a story. Not to mention the fact that many forms of short fiction are also indigenous, whereas the novel is an imported form.

In fact, at least in Marathi, about which I can say a little, the past half-century has seen a great and definite production of country short fiction. Starting with the work of a small number of essentially urban(ised) writers, it has now progressed to a stage at which, from every region and sub-region, caste and sub-caste and dwindling forest tribe, writers are practising the art of the short story. So considerable is this production that at times it suggests a glut. But it does seem to me that a form which is easier to complete, easier to publish, that may appear in a variety of organs from journals, magazines and even newspapers, to anthologies—a form written by 'those who know,' which vividly inscribes a people's history and not merely a dry, feelingless, statistical record or even a rarefied, sophisticated, distanced 'literary' record—has been adopted by Marathi country writers. There is justification—if you see the threatened country ethos the way I do—for recommending the writing of the country short story in other languages in which such writing has not happened. (I use Marathi as an instance; I would indeed be surprised if similar cases did not obtain at least in a few other Indian languages.)

Now, turning to our immediate concern here, the role of English in all this inscriptional activity needs to be examined and constructive possibilities outlined. My ideas come from personal experience and are valid to the extent that my perceptions are fair. Modifications and corrections to them are, needless to say, welcome.

In some ways, the less we say about Indian Writing in English in *this* context the better. Little has been achieved there so far in the interest of the Indian countryside, and writers today (and even Indian critics following them) seem bent on further urbanisation. Suffice it to say that anyone with a foot in the countryside, a genuine feel for it, and both creative talent and adequate English can, of course, write country stories in English.

The major role for English, however, happens to be predictable. In English translation Indian country writing can be disbursed to both Indian and non-Indian readers. Else, indeed, English can be dismissed.

Here, I will concentrate on just one aspect of the business of translating and publishing translated country short stories in English. That is, the language of translation. In this connection, both translators and publishers have certain fundamental and serious responsibilities. First, the translators. It is possible that there are a few people in the countryside who possess the right kind of English to render country matters and flavours into English. Chances are heavily against such as a case, though. Equally, those who ought to know better, in a variety of English-based professions in India including our own, have neglected both the Indian countryside and the English (or American, Australian, etc.) countryside in their pursuit of either aggressive westernisation of their language for use in commerce and the hinterland of commerce in urban and international settings, or ever highly specialised varieties of literary and theoretical registers of English. Neither English curricula nor private reading seem to include country-related materials in English. Add to this the predictable problem that English country registers may not apply to or serve Indian country matters without undergoing creative transformation, and also the problem (a reality) that practically all users of English in India command only a bookishly formal, more or less unidiomatic and urban English. It seems clear that despite substantial country writing at least in some Indian languages, we may lack the wherewithal for engaging in the necessary task of translating it into appropriate English. Further, without going into technical socio-linguistic detail, it should be fairly obvious to everyone that, already, country language is always substantially diferent from urban language within even the monolinguistic situation. Besides this, along with country phenomena, a good part of these country dialects is also disappearing. This is probably also the place to note that to render creative country materials into deadpan, bookish, flatly formal, urban English would amount to grave violence.

Briefly, given this situation, the publishing industry is even less prepared for the task of producing volumes of such writing in the right spirit of adventure and imaginative openness to creative effort made by translators. Indeed, it is my own experience that publishers may be actually antipathetic to such creative effort, and in favour of what they are pleased to call 'standard' English. Having looked at the situation of 'rural', 'grameen' or 'country' writing in Marathi for a paper some time back (Marathe 1992) I proposed to a publisher that it would make sense to put together a volume of stories by one of the earliest country writers in Marathi. The entire work was finished a year and a half ago; two promised publication dates have gone by; and the publisher has not only attempted to make unwarranted 'editorial' alterations (when I am in fact the editor) but also inserted about 1000 equally unwarranted textual changes in the translation of 11 short stories. The only 'explanation' offered is that the publisher has done a lot of work 'in the interest of standard English,' which neither the original author nor I are willing to accept.

A pioneering volume has been, in this way, inordinately delayed. In fact the publisher sought to make these changes 'silently', without as much as a by-your-leave. In the entire episode, I can only say that the high points have been the author's confidence and the approval of all those who have read the translations.

But, apart from publishers, even colleagues may pose problems. I was once asked to translate early nineteenth century 'romantic' poetry from Marathi into English; when I protested, saying that I was not familiar enough with either the texts, or the ethos of the period or the language of that poetry, a friend's response was—'How long are you going to keep that "mask" on?' The end of that story was pleasant, however, because that friend and his co-editor for the Sahitya Akademi volume accepted my proposal that I translate those poems in collaboration with a sensitive Marathi scholar.

If translate we must—and I have suggested that in the interest of preserving an *affectively* vivid record of the vanishing country life of India we need to do so, if not also as an act of social justice—then what ought we to do?

1. Those of us who have the opportunity should start, deliberately, reading country writing in our own languages and exploring the matrices of life recorded in it.
2. We should start reading country writing in English (i.e. British, American, Commonwealth, etc., writing done by those whose language is English, or those who have successfully appropriated it for indigenous and non-urban subject matter).
3. We should start teaching, as a matter of course, samples of country writing in our programmes.
4. There is a species of English writing, doubtless with its own problems, about the Indian countryside by outsiders (e.g., Rudyard Kipling, Philip Mason, a host of Anglo-Indians); this writing may be creative or documentary, but it has made some effort already to bend the English language into application to Indian country life; we should study this aspect of such writing and cull from it any linguistic-stylistic means that we may find useful.
5. Special country dialectal variations, at least in lexical terms and basic grammatical terms, have not been strictly or exhaustively recorded in modern dictionaries and grammars of our own languages. A non-country translator is hamstrung without lexical-grammatical aids that help him out with country usage. We should make some effort, therefore, at least via translation, to discover and record country usage, and its equivalents in English need to be either found or created. In fact, it may make sense to put all translations into a data bank from which other translators can draw English equivalents for usages in their own country dialects. Translators must not only endeavour to arrive at passable country alternatives in English, but they must also collaborate across languages in a sort of country-dictionary project.
6. We should make an effort to create publication possibilities for trial translations so that this work may be shared and refined. For instance, private circulation avenues should be created; the Sahitya Akademi ought to regularly provide space in its journals for publication of trial material from

which really accomplished items can be published again, after refinement, in *Indian Literature*.

I shall assume that my list of tasks may be extended by others. Let me, therefore, turn to one or two specific problems which commercial publishers are likely to create. First of all, they may not quite understand that there will be a sizeable readership for volumes of translated country stories within India. Next, they do not seem to understand the value of *creation* of an appropriate English for such translation (indeed, they may actually meddle with a translator's text); they seem not to have noticed that there is a large readership outside India for such interestingly venturesome material; that users of English are anyhow already extending their reading beyond so-called standard usage by reading translations from *other* languages; that what is called 'standard' English in India is one of the weakest, most colourless and lifeless varieties of English, which itself may benefit from the infusion of vigour from translations of country stories. Further, they do not seem to seize the opportunity created by the development-oriented English readership in India which is short of time but would take kindly to shorter fiction about life outside their own pale if only it were made available in English from the many Indian languages.

Whatever I have suggested here may apply to poetry and longer fiction but I do believe that the short story is the form most successfully used at least in Marathi country writing; besides, poetry has always had a smaller readership, and longer fiction (again at least in Marathi country literature) has yet to succeed in transcending essentially autobiographical narration. I hope that in this paper I have provided some useful indications of the tasks and responsibilities, relating to the country short story in India, that some of us in English Studies ought to consider ours.

Works Cited

Marathe, Sudhakar. 1992. 'Madgulkar's *Bangarwadi*, Rural India in Marathi and the Case of English.' *Images of Rural India in the Twentieth Century*. Eds. Alok Bhalla and Peter Bumke. New Delhi: Sterling. 262–76.

Meshram, Bhujang. 1990. *Ulgulan*. Kalyan: Tathagat Prakashan.

Of Other Voices: Mahasweta Devi's Short Stories Translated by Gayatri Chakravorty Spivak

TUTUN MUKHERJEE

The short story has, along with the film, greatly altered the conventional notions of the narrative. The genre is the typical product of an age which is not amenable to drawn-out yarns, excursive explanations or orientation with any one all-encompassing story. It lends itself admirably to the presentation of the partial, the incomplete and that which cannot be organised or explained satisfactorily. The short story, offering varieties and contingencies of situations, zeroes in on the moments of crises which never fail to convey a degree of mystery, elision, or the uncertainty of the unexplored.

But, surprisingly, the short story as a genre, has not been given the distinction it deserves. The critical negligence or complacency it has been subjected to may be due to two factors: first, an elitist bias encouraged by the banal way the short story used to reach the reader: via pedestrian magazines, anthologies and miscellanies; second, the presupposition that the various types of fiction operated with principles very much the same and so the short story could be subsumed generally under fiction. In fact, Henry James (1962) had expressed certain reservations about the brevity of the short story which, he feared, was achieved at the expense of some other literary value. On the other hand, in the postmodern era of 'blurred genres' or 'non-genres' (Geertz 1980:167) when the focus is on the 'text' and 'ecriture'—the metonyms for literature indicating the transgression of all genetic boundaries, any claim for the generic distinction of the short story would surely seem self-defeating. However, according to Derrida, while the avoidance of generic classifications seeks to abolish the hierarchies of the prescriptive classical theories which assume the fixity of genres along with the social and literary authority such limits exert in an attempt 'to order the manifold within a nomenclature,' other trajectories are definitely possible (Derrida 1980:208). The postmodern aim is to effect an interface of the trivial and the ignored genres in culture and the canonised genres. The need of the time is to minimise classification and maximise clarification and analysis.

It is not easy to formulate a theory of the short story because of the immense potential of its thematic and stylistic variations. But it is necessary to mark the short story as qualitatively different from the novel. It should not be dismissed as a story told short nor condemned with the praise of its logical and coherent unity! The brevity of the short story entails a compact intensity of language and style, a concentration of mood and events incorporating the inchoate, an element of suggestiveness and surprise. It is also possible to identify other genetic traces it has derived from the epistemic transformations (of socio-cultural contexts and political agendas). The short story has very often served as the vehicle for different kinds of knowledge which may be at odds with the story of the dominant culture. The short story is the awareness of the complex interweave of independent stories peripheral or palimpsest to the ruling, organising epistemological narrative. It is, therefore, 'a form of the margins, ex-centric, not a part of the official or high-cultural hegemony' (Hanson 1989:2, 6).

The short story in its modern form developed in India during the turbulent times of the freedom struggle and also marked a crucial moment in the history of Indian letters. It was nurtured by the events of national insurgence and has since then remained a mode for expressing the suppressed/repressed. However, the short fictional pieces which filled the magazines, literary journals and anthologies till 1910 were mostly historical and mythological tales and legends, travel adventures and stories about Indian manners and ceremonies: all peddling festishised oriental exotica (Naik 1992:109–10). It was only in the context of the intensifying socio-political and ideological ferment in the country that the short story matured. It is significant that the short story remained for long a neglected and wandering trace within the exclusive and exclusionary aesthetic conception of literature. Needless to say, this totalised concept of literature, a masterful narrative containment within 'a few selective, authoritative, "authentic" textualities', was a deliberate Orientalist attempt at constructing a monolithic racio-cultural identity of the country, deliberately eliding over the 'mosaic of diverse social, cultural and religious formations and realities' (Joshi 1994:15–16) in an attempt to construct a nation modelled on the Western concept—that is, 'the other as Self's Shadow' (Spivak 1988)—and also to inscribe a monological narrative of reality as the normative one. According to Timothy Brennan, 'nations [are] imaginary constructs that depend for their existence on the apparatus of cultural fictions in which imaginative literature plays a decisive role' (Brennan 1990:49). Brennan says that this role of nation-building has been played by the novel which is able to accommodate the enormous cultural heterogeneity of social formations within its specific narrative form. A corroboration of this view is Benedict Anderson's comment (as quoted in Brennan) that the novel depicts 'the movement of a solitary hero through a sociological landscape of *fixity that fuses* the world inside the novel with the world outside' (50: emphasis mine). As has been argued by many cultural historians, 'haunting [the] large and liminal image' of the nation and the monological discourse of nationhood, are many 'textual strategies, metaphoric displacements, subtext and figurative stratagems' which help to explore the 'deep nation—the long past' as the threshold of meaning that needs to be 'crossed, erased and translated in the process of cultural production' (Bhabha 1990:2–3). It is also a fact that the selective incorporation and the translation of canonised texts formed a foundational part of the Orientalist project as did the exemplification of 'traditional' poets and novelists (occluding the short story writer) and thus established the system of literary and cultural valorisation.

It will be too sweeping a generalisation if I say that the short story as a mode of expression succeeded in effecting a rupture in the process of narrativising a nation. However, it will be appropriate to review the short story, written in the vernaculars rather than in English, as the 'embattled space of struggle' against the prescriptive and proscribing literary and cultural codes. This space is filled with stories that disturb, assault, wrench and disrupt our thoughts, as for instance the stories of Premchand, Vatsyayan, Premendra Mitra, Buddhadeb Bose, Manik Bandyopadhyay, Ismat Chugtai or Manto. Their engagement is with life: to address the unconventional, the unacknowledged, the deviant; to map histories, human relations and meanings; to weave the strands of submerged narrativities into the texture of literature. Theirs is also a struggle with language and style as they try to forge a dynamic, stark and effective prose.

The focus of my paper is one such site of struggle: the short stories of Mahasweta Devi translated by Gayatri Chakravorty Spivak. I refer specifically to three stories: 'Draupadi' (Spivak 1987), 'Stanadayini' (Spivak 1987), and 'Shikar' (Spivak 1993a).

Mahasweta Devi's collection of short narratives, *Agnigarbha* (Womb of Fire) appeared when she had already marked her path with her novels. In her novels, she inscribes those fiery moments of subaltern rebellion as the space of 'the displacement of the colonisation-decolonisation reversal' (Spivak 1993b:79) which had been effected from cultural memory by the sanctioned ignorance of history. Her short stories delve into the recesses of cultural memory and describe her 'secret encounters with singular figures' (Spivak 1993a:199) and bring to focus the subliminal traces of exploitation that had, no doubt, stoked the fire of such rebellion. For the world in general, 'India' very often serves as a monolithic concept/label which conceals immense and unacknowledged heterogeneities. According to Spivak, 'Mahasweta releases that heterogeneity, restoring some of its historical and geographical nomenclature' (Spivak, 1993b:79). The short stories become the subtexts that assign new meanings to the processes of historical change.

All the three short stories, taken up for discussion here, sketch the gendered subject enmeshed in the lateral mappings and relationships which reveal the cartography of power and social control. Significantly, the naming of the three protagonists—Draupadi, Jashoda, Mary—stirs mythic memories and their subject-representation and constitution is deliberately palimpsest and contradictory. Draupadi, the heroine of the epic *Mahabharata*, is a unique and exceptional woman, married to five husbands, yet odd and unpaired: *nathbati anathbat*. She 'provides the occasion for a violent transaction between men' and becomes the 'efficient cause' of the crucial battle (Spivak 1987:183). An unforgettable episode in the epic is the attempt made by the enemy chief to disrobe Draupadi.

But there is the miraculous intervention of the divine law-giver and Draupadi is infinitely clothed and cannot be publicly stripped. Dopdi (the tribal form of the Sanskrit name) in Mahasweta Devi's story is stripped and gang-raped as punishment for her political misdemeanour and impertinence. Dopdi refuses to put on her 'cloth' as she mocks the law-giver, Senanayak: 'You can strip me but how can you clothe me again?' (Spivak 1987:196)

Mahasweta Devi always avoids the blandness of the ubiquitous term 'harijan' and not only describes the tribal affiliation of every subaltern character but also the unclean menial task that places each untouchable in the rigid social classification. The rhetoric of prejudice contained in the caste name is impossible to convey through translation.

Jashoda is the mythic all-nurturing Mother-figure, the Divine Mother suckling the Holy Child. According to Spivak, Mahasweta Devi's Jashoda is an interpellation into the patriarchal ideology which is conveyed ironically by the title, 'Stanadayini', that means not 'the suckler' but rather 'the giver of the breast' and clearly 'alienates' the 'means of production, the part object, the distinguishing organ of the female as mother' (Spivak 1987:250, 267). Spivak adds that,

> Mahasweta introduces exploitation/domination into that detail in the mythic story which tells us that Jashoda is a foster-mother. By turning fostering into a profession, she sees mothering in its materiality beyond its socialisation as affect, beyond psychologisation as abjection, or yet transcendentalisation as the vehicle of the divine (264).

There are many narrative frames within the story. Within the ideological and nationalist frame, Jashoda may also be taken as the image of India as the foster-mother to those who exploit her and feed upon her body politic and then reject and deny her. As the final act of violence upon abject Motherhood, Jashoda's corpse lies unclaimed in the mortuary of a general hospital with only a name tag, 'Jashoda, Hindu female.'

Mary Oraon of 'The Hunt' is the only protagonist who lets violence ricochet off her. She becomes the aggressor and, activating a tribal ritual as an expression of resistance, turns the exploiter into the ritual prey. Is this possible because there is the white man's gene in her? The act of violence also marks the parabolic path of her name from the ancient site of another sacrifice.

Mary carves a niche of exclusivity for herself and uses the very notion of her mixed blood to her advantage in her negotiations with the resources of the other side. She is meticulous about claiming her dues in return for her labour.

Mahasweta Devi is not just fictionalising subaltern history or recording events from the outside. She is fascinated by the individual in history and her own involvement with the indigenous tribal people of Chotanagpur is total. In her conversation with Spivak, she says,

> ...my involvement started long ago. In 1965, I started going to Palamu. Of course my mental involvement was already there. I was interested in them, but did not know very much... when I understood that feeling for the tribals and writing about them was not enough, I started living with them (Spivak 1993a:iv).

She understood the plight of the Sobors, a common name for the dispossessed hunting tribes of Palamu, Chaibasa, Chhattisgarh and Purulia. The British government had isolated such small tribes who lived off the forest and did not take to cultivation. The forests were claimed as agricultural land or protected area and the tribals were branded criminals and poachers. Their treatment by the Government of independent India was no different. The tribes were denotified and ostracised as criminals. They were indeed used and abused in criminal activities, in flesh trade, and as bonded labour. The changing times demanded that they too change the pattern of their lives. But how were they to do so without help? However, any help that is offered to the indigenous tribals, should come as an acknowledgement of their rights. To understand their needs and their demands would mean accepting their claims upon their land which would then necessitate the re-examination of the processes of colonisation and decolonisation in a new perspective, that is, a re-writing of history!

In their path-breaking book recording the ecological history of India, Madhav Gadgil and Ramachandra Guha (1993:177) write,

> Researches over the past two decades have quite convincingly demonstrated that while the peasant operates in a world largely composed of 'illiterates,' and consequently many peasant movements lack a written manifesto, his actions are imbued with a certain rationality and internally consistent system of values.

Gadgil and Guha emphasise that it is the task of the scholar to 'reconstruct this ideology' that is sometimes articulated as explicit episodes of revolt but more implicitly informs the peasant's everyday existence. The historians maintain that the tribals' protests against 'enforced social and ecological changes clearly articulate a sophisticated theory of resource use that had both political and cultural overtones' (177).

The tribals worship nature and before felling a tree or killing an animal to appease their simple wants, they pray to the spirit of the forest for forgiveness. They have no concept of property or money. The tribals do not denude forests. It is big money that is involved in the deforestation scam. The modern world neither understands the tribal sensibility nor appreciates what the tribal wants. Mahasweta Devi symbolises the tribal as the pre-historic pterodactyl. There is no way of establishing contact or communication with the pterodactyl to know the message it wishes to convey. Yet, ironically, 'the tribals and the mainstream have always been parallel. There has never been a meeting point. The mainstream simply doesn't understand the parallel' (Spivak 1993a:ii).

Mahasweta Devi immersed herself in the rehabilitation work of the Sobors. She also wrote a lot at the same time, giving exposure to the plight of the tribals in her own journal, *Bartika*, and in the newspaper columns that she regularly wrote; she pestered the central and state administrations and 'fought' for projects and funds; in 1986, she spearheaded the formation of Tribal Unity Forum (*Adim Jati Aikya Parishad*) to preclude 'the disunity among the tribals that the system wants' (Spivak 1993a:ix).

Mahasweta Devi's stories are an extension of her activism and her reportage. Her intention is not to romanticise the tribals and give them a heroic life within the sealed subjectivity of her fiction but to imaginatively recreate their lives by transgressing the boundaries of life and fiction. She draws upon her experience with them and her knowledge of their philosophy of living—each life a confirmation of courage, wisdom and endurance. The stories are linked together with the common thread of profound ecological loss, the loss of the forest as foundation of life and also, as Spivak insists, with the 'complicity,' however remote, 'of the power lines of local developers with the forces of global capital' (Spivak 1993a:201).

But what compels her? Mahasweta Devi says:

> I think a creative writer should have a social consciousness. I have a duty toward society. Yet I don't really know why I do these things. This sense of duty is an obsession and I must remain accountable to myself. I ask myself this question a thousand times: have I done what I could have done? (Spivak 1993a:ix).

Spivak describes this as Mahasweta Devi's 'unusual ethical responsiveness.' Her writing and her activism reflect one another in a kind of 'folding back upon one another…a reflection in the root sense [of] permanent persuasion' (Spivak 1993a:xxii).

By taking up the task of translating Mahasweta Devi's short stories, Spivak ensures their inclusion among the narratives of colonial resistance. However, this task implicates the translator-commentator in the strongly nuanced site of struggle. There are at least two ways of addressing the problematics of articulating resistance; on the level of literature and on the level of language.

In a sweeping statement, Frederic Jameson writes (1986:68–69):

> What all third world cultural productions seem to have in common and what distinguishes them radically from analogous cultural forms in the first world is that all third world texts are necessarily allegorical, and in a very specific way they are to be read as what I will call national allegories.

Besides the reductive categorisation of 'third world literature', Jameson imposes a further restriction that no other category besides 'nation' can offer viable modes for interpreting literature, totally negating such perspectives as gender, class, ethnicity, race, culture or language. Spivak's theme is large: the micro-politics of 'nation-hood' and its relation to the macro-narrative of 'imperialism'. Spivak is aware that the attempt to understand subaltern classes only in terms of their first-world models is deeply destructive. Her programme demands that the subaltern not be confined as a historiographical trace or even as a literary trope, but be encouraged to speak, allowing its consciousness to find a mode of expression that can inflect and produce forms of political liberation displacing the occidental concepts of nation. She 'elaborates' Mahasweta Devi's texts which focus upon the gendered subaltern's body, abused and exploited with unutterable ugliness and cruelty. But Dopdi, Doulati and Jashoda do not remain silent signifiers. They speak with their bodies and that rhetoric is as violent as Mary Oraon's enactment of the ancient ritual of Janiparab by killing her tormentor. According to Colin MacCabe, 'the analyst of culture must be able to sketch the real effects of the imaginary in her object of study while never forgetting the imaginary effects of the real in her own investigation' (MacCabe 1987:xvi). Spivak understands the real as the excess of the female body which must be placed in its cultural and economic specificity to provoke the imaginary figuration.

Another consideration involves the conflictual topos of language and the problematic role of the translator trying to engender the Ur text. The conventional view of translation expects the translator to produce a version of the original in the target language that reads well and sounds right and, at the same time, to interpret and re-produce the messages of the original faithfully. What I wish to emphasise here is that translation, when it occurs, has to carry over whatever meaning it has grasped from the original into another framework that tends to impose not only a different set of discursive relations but also reveals interstices of tension. Therefore difference must be the acknowledged quality of all translations. Moreover, to say that translation is always already interpretation is not enough. An adequate translation has to incorporate two interpretations or a double interpretation requiring double writing which is like the 'pluralised dislocutory paralogical writing practice that Derrida has so often cultivated and explained' (Lewis 1985:44). Derrida's experiments with double-edged writing is in response to the need for two interpretations, 'one in compliance with the target language and the other in realignment with the original text' in the form of commentary. Spivak fills the space between the original and her translation with her commentary. Her intention is to effect an epistemic transformation of the concept of the monolithic 'third-world woman' by drawing attention to the mechanics of investigating the subaltern consciousness. Her practice problematises the use of English for retrieving the socio-economic dynamics of postcolonial narratives. The language and style of Mahasweta Devi's short stories instantiate her resistance to both the heavily Sanskritised idiom and the sentimental idiom prevalent in contemporary writings. She puts together an effective prose that is 'a collage of literary Bengali, street Bengali, bureaucratic Bengali, tribal Bengali and the language of the tribals' (Spivak 1987:180). She leaves the sprinkling of pidgin English as is used in general colloquy. The style is direct and frank. She is often accused of writing 'like a man' (Mukherjee 1991:31). Her stories are meticulously researched and annotated, with no glossing-over of facts.

Bengali is a left branching language in its clause and sentence structure. Usually, the verb comes at the end of the clause of the sentence. The translation of a sentence in Bengali necessitates the reading of it as a unity and not word by word. Moreover, Bengali is not a highly inflected language in which case-endings and so on would make the relationships between words obvious. In fact, it is a language in which great subtleties are made possible with syntactic variations.

Mahasweta Devi's prose is certainly a challenge to any translator, made more so by the rhetorical specificity of her writing. For instance, not distinguishing between reported and indirect speech is a remarkable way of conflating the outer and the inner enclaves. The gap between the writer and the native informer is erased. It becomes the translator's task to convey the closeness of this bonding.

Spivak avoids meddling with dialects and translates in

'straight' English. But she has been criticised for using the language of American academia 'not sufficiently accessible' to Indian readers. This raises the interesting debate about the characteristics of 'Indian-English' and the translator's struggle to meet the cultural expectations of the implied readers of distinctive blocs as 'Indian literature' and 'World literature'. Spivak tries to undo such divisions to allow the 'collaborative/parasitical/contrary/resistant relationship' between literatures to surface in literary and cultural dialectics (Spivak 1993c:142).

As for the questions of loss in translation, Spivak (1993a:xxvi) quotes J.M. Coetzee's comments:

> It is in the nature of the literary work to present its translator with problems for which the perfect solution is impossible.... There is never enough closeness of fit between languages for formal features of a work to be mapped across from one language to another without shift of value...something must be 'lost'...

What Spivak succeeds in conveying are the 'secret encounters with the singular figures' of Mahasweta Devi's stories, maintaining as closely as possible the specificities of language, theme and history. Furthermore, according to Spivak (1993b:77):

> The sheer quantity of Mahasweta's production, her preoccupation with the gendered subaltern subject, and the range of her experimental prose—moving from the tribal to the Sanskritic register by way of easy obscenity and political analysis—will not permit her to be an isolated voice.

Giving Mahasweta Devi's work the *anushilan*—that is, close-reading, attention, concentration—that it deserves, Spivak, invoking Gramsci, constructs a dialectical space for organic intellectuals. When the subaltern 'speaks', it is 'in order to be heard and be admitted into the structure of responsible (responding and being responded to) resistance and he or she is or is on the way to becoming an organic intellectual' (Spivak 1993a:xxi). Listening and responding to the Other Voices speaking in Mahasweta Devi's short stories would indeed create just such a community of organic intellectuals.

Works Cited

Bhabha, Homi K. (ed.). 1990.'Introduction: Narrating the Nation.' *Nation and Narration*. London: Routledge. 1–7.

Brennan, Timothy. 1990. 'The National Longing for Form.' Homi K. Bhabha (ed.). *Nation and Narration*. London: Routledge.

Derrida, Jacques. 1980. 'The Law of the Genre.' *Glyph*. 7. Baltimore & London: John Hopkins University Press. 176–232.

Gadgil, Madhav and Ramchandra Guha. 1993. *This Fissured Land: An Ecological History of India*. Delhi: Oxford University Press.

Geertz, Clifford. 1980. 'Blurred Genres: The Refiguration of Social Thought.' *The American Scholar*. 49. 165–79.

Hanson, Clare. (ed). 1989. 'Introduction.' *Rereading the Short Story*. New York: St. Martin's Press. 1–9.

James, Henry. 1962. 'Definitions and Discriminations.' J.E. Miller Jr. (ed). *Theory of Fiction*. Lincoln: University of Nebraska Press. 99–104.

Jameson, Frederic. 1986. 'Third World Literature in an Era of Multinational Capitalism.' *Social Text*. 15. 65–88.

Joshi, Svati (ed). 1994. 'Introduction.' *Rethinking English*. Delhi: Oxford University Press. 31–62.

MacCabe, Colin. 1987. 'Preface.' In Gayatri Chakravorty Spivak: *In Other Worlds: Essays in Cultural Politics*. New York & London: Methuen. i–xx.

Mukherjee, Sujit. 1991. Review of *In Other Worlds*. *Book Review*. XIV. 3. May-June. 31.

Naik, M.K. 1992. *History of Indian English Literature*. New Delhi: Sahitya Akademi.

Spivak, Gayatri Chakravorty. 1987. *In Other Worlds: Essays in Cultural Politics*. New York & London: Methuen.

—. 1988. 'Can the Subaltern Speak?' Cary Nelson and Lawrence Grossberg (eds). *Marxism and the Interpretation of Culture*. Urbana and Chicago: University of Illinois Press. 271–313.

—. 1993a. *Imaginary Maps*. Calcutta: Thema.

—. 1993b. *Outside in the Teaching Machine*. New York and London: Routledge.

—. 1993c. 'The Burden of English.' C. Breckenridge & P. Van Der Veer (eds.). *Orientalism and the Post-Colonial Predicament*. Delhi: Oxford University Press. 134–157.

Male Culture, Female Strategies

RANJANA HARISH

> Women will starve in silence until new stories are created which confer on them the power of naming themselves.
>
> Sandra Gilbert and Susan Gubar

The gynocritical ideal of the 'world proper' in which women writers create a literature of their own, has been a world allowing centrality to them and conferring on them the power of naming. However, one knows that the world proposed by these critics is an utopia. One also knows that women, though lacking new stories have not really starved in silence. Living in male culture they have invented female strategies for survival as well as for self-expression.

The very fact that women inhabit a world dominated by male culture gives them a special gender identity (a psycho-social construct) the encoding of which begins much earlier than that of sex identity (the biological category). According to Nancy Chodorow (1978), a psychoanalyst whose work has had an enormous influence on women's studies in the west, the gender-based identity formation of women as a marginalised class exercises a deep influence on their creative writing. It is all the more so in the Indian set-up where in Sudhir Kakar's view even the bedtime stories about mythological characters like Sita and Savitri carry 'seeds of deep-rooted acculturation' for Indian girls (Kakar 1978:15).

In a patriarchal culture which does not allow much space to women and which appreciates women better in their 'muted' state, asserting their individuality by writing is a difficult task for women. They may carve out a safe space for themselves by creating typical 'feminine' texts of domestic bliss and fantasies. But when the creative urge in them compels them to transgress these and other prescribed feminine boundaries and urges them to tackle unconventional subjects which move against the cultural current, women writers experience agoraphobia. Their gender-based need for acceptance, in Carolyn Heilbrun's view, makes them invent strategies—thematic, narrative as well as linguistic. Heilbrun in her famous book *Writing a Woman's Life* (1988) discusses women writers' strategies in detail.

Compared to 'theory', a strategy is something much more personal. Often it is a device invented on a personal level to cope with certain situations, and is similar to strategies in war or in a game. Choosing to discuss women writers' strategies does not imply that men writers do not employ any strategies. But the strategies used by women are indeed very different, as the cultural determinants play a very important part in devising them.

My argument in this paper is that in the absence of any well-defined theory of tradition of women's writing in male culture, women writers often invent strategies to cope with two opposite pulls—their creative urge for self-expression which means the cultivation of the ego on the one hand, and their need for acceptance in a patriarchal set-up which means the curbing or submergence of the female ego on the other. And as in life so in literature, they carve out their space with typical feminine skill and grace by inventing different strategies to suit different situations.

This paper proposes to study thematic, narrative and linguistic strategies employed by two Indian women short story writers—Indira Goswami (Assamese) and Dina Mehta (English) in their respective stories 'The Offspring' and 'And No Birds Sing'. Indira Goswami's story is translated by the writer herself. Dina Mehta's is in English. Thus we have the writers' own English in these stories which justifies the discussion about their linguistic strategies also.

A short story, to quote Walter Allen, is 'the fruit of a single moment of time, of a single incident, a single perception' (Allen 1981:7). From this viewpoint the 'single perception' which is revealed in 'The Offspring' and 'And No Birds Sing' is the feminine perception. Both of these are the stories of women's experiences in men's world, of women's survival strategies in a male dominated culture, of 'patterns if not universal, at least, very widespread in female experience' to quote Patricia Meyer Spacks (1975:5). They are the outcome of the writer's first-hand experience of a woman's life. It is this first-hand experience of the women writers themselves, of being pushed to the margins, and of being muted constantly, which gives their rendering of such 'feminine situations' in literature an authenticity. According to Simone de Beauvoir (1953) there is no feminine nature, there is only a 'feminine situation' which has remained constant through centuries.

'The Offspring' is the story of a middle aged man's yearning for a child. Pitambar Mahajan is a rich childless pariah of a small village. Pitambar has married a second wife, who has been bedridden for months by the time the story begins. The husband is sad, he is sorry, not for his dying wife but for the fact that the 'barren woman' would leave him without an offspring. The priest of the village always reminds him of his 'duty' to have a male child to 'continue the family name'. Pitambar's sense of having failed in his manly duty has given him a complex. He always talks to others 'with averted eyes and a bowed head' (Goswami 1992:11). Finally the priest suggests a solution. Why not think of Damayanti, 'the young widow of a priest?' She is available. Pitambar can have a child by her. What an idea! Pitambar is thrilled. But will it be possible? 'Yes why not? If you want you can make Damayanti your own,' says the priest. But what about the difference in their caste the Pariah man hesitates. 'Who cares? Nowadays Brahmin girls are even marrying fishermen' is the priest's argument.

It is all settled between the men. The priest will persuade Damayanti. Right at that time Damayanati passes that way. She is young. She is beautiful. And she is a widow—i.e. no man's possession. Both the middle-aged men stare at her with their hungry eyes. The writer describes the scene thus:

> Her blouse had stretched tight and was pulled up, revealing the white flesh which to the two men looked as tempting as the meat dressed and hung up on iron hooks in a butcher's shop

The priest tries to talk to her but ignoring him she just walks away. Angered by her lack of reverence for him, the highly respected priest of the village temple, the priest pours out his indignation: 'This girl has brought disgrace to Brahmins. She has thrown to the winds all restraints and rituals prescribed for widows' (12). Yes, agrees Pitambar. He has even heard that many men and college boys visit her. The priest adds to the information that she has gone through four abortions and 'every time she has buried those evil things in the bamboo grove behind her house' (13). Who would ever care for such a slut? Yes, nobody should. And yet Pitambar definitely would.

A few days later, the priest informs Pitambar that Damayanti's womb is empty. If Pitambar agrees to spend good money he can arrange for an offspring. After all it is a question of prime importance in the male world—a male offspring. The deal is settled.

Pitambar sets out for Damayanti's house on a full moon night. He looks up at the moonlit sky and fantasises. The moon becomes Damayanti's body. He imagines the shape of her breast which would be like 'the soft rounded stomach of a pregnant goat' (18). He is more interested in her pregnancy than in her female body. She sees him and holds out a candle with a sharp question, 'Have you brought some money?' He is stunned. He realises that this is the first time she has opened her mouth. 'Whatever I have is yours,' he says, and hands over his purse to her.

Some time later the priest brings the news that Damayanti is pregnant. Pitambar jumps up with joy. His dreams have come true at last. He becomes insane with happiness and pleads with the priest to convince Damayanti not to destroy the foetus this time. If she agrees to bear the child he will marry her; he will do whatever she says. Three months pass without any bad news. Now nobody, neither his friends, nor wife, nor even Damayanti matter to him. The only one who matters is 'the youthful son of his hallucinations'. This happy trance is broken by the priest on a very stormy night. In the torrential rain Pitambar hears somebody calling out his name. His heart sinks with apprehension. Who could it be? Looking out he finds the priest standing in the rain, soaked to the skin. He tells Pitambar that Damayanti has destroyed the foetus.

Next night, when the rain and storm subside, Damayanti

hears the sound of digging in her backyard. Looking through the window she finds Pitambar digging the ground where the foetus was buried. She is horrified. She runs out shouting. 'What will you get there? Yes, I have buried it! It was a boy! But he is just a lump of flesh, blood and mud! Stop it.'

The broken-hearted father cries out, 'I'll touch that flesh with these hands of mine. He was the scion of my lineage, a part of my flesh and blood. I will touch him.'

On the surface, 'The Offspring' is a man's story—about a man's desire for male offspring. Narratologically too it is a story told in the third person from a male point of view. And yet it is not simply a man's point of view. It is not a man's story in the usual sense as it comes from a woman's pen. Choosing a male-centered situation and highlighting it in the title, choosing a male dominated set-up and rendering the heroine mute can be interpreted as a strategic move on the part of the woman story writer. From a gynocentric point of view, this thematic strategy works at two levels—at the level of the story-teller, where it affords a 'double-voiced discourse' to borrow Showalter's term, and at the level of the female protagonist, Damayanti, where the strategies adopted by her to handle her life help her to cope with the particular 'feminine situation'. Hidden behind her inarticulate, non-responsive feminine strategy is a self who knows how to assert her power over her body.

'Double-voiced discourse', a term coined by Showalter, describes the thematic strategy that women resort to in the face of an oppressive and silencing male culture. Showalter (1981:204) sees this as a surivival strategy and observes:

> Women's fiction can be read as a double-voiced discourse, containing a 'dominant' and a 'muted' story, what Gilbert and Gubar call a 'palimpsest'. I have described it elsewhere as an object/field problem in which we must keep two alternative oscillating texts simultaneously in view.... The orthodox plot recedes, and another plot, hitherto submerged in the anonymity of the background, stands out in bold relief like a thumbprint. Miller too sees 'another text' in women's fiction, 'more or less muted from novel to novel' but 'always there to be read'.

Indira Goswami's 'The Offspring' can be read as a

double-voiced discourse containing a dominant and a muted story—the dominant theme of male desire for offspring and the muted theme of female survival in a male world. The writer presents the muted side of the theme with typical feminine silences, gaps and blanks—'the holes in the discourse' to use Showalter's phrase (193). Damayanti knows that she is looked upon as a commodity, an object of pleasure and a means of attaining an offspring for Pitambar. But she does not react to all this in words. Her silence however does not mean that she is not strong. It suggests instead that she knows that as a woman, and a widow at that, she cannot afford to be articulate. Throughout the story there are only two occasions when she opens her mouth, once to ask for money when Pitambar comes to her hut, and the other time to stop him from digging out the foetus from her backyard. One other instance is when her words are reported to Pitambar by the priest, namely that she will not entertain Pitambar as he is a low caste man. That is all. But in all these three instances when her muted self acquires articulation we see her as a person who knows her mind. She knows what she is doing and why. She is aware of the reality that in the male world women are loved for their utility and every utilitarian object has its price, so why hesitate in fixing one's price? She needs money to survive. Being a Brahmin woman she may dislike the idea of entertaining a low caste man. But her worldly wisdom tells her that one always has to make compromises to survive. She may purify her defiled body by taking a bath after he leaves. Once again a strategy! She is actually found taking a bath at the well after Pitambar leaves. But when it comes to giving birth to a pariah's child she is firm. She will do no such thing. It is her body and she exercises her power over her body. She cannot be lured into motherhood by the bait of marriage.

Dina Mehta's 'And No Birds Sing' (1992) provides a good illustration of how in women's stories, the subplot, a usual narrative technique, acquires a special meaning. Often in handling a double-voiced discourse women writers take the help of narratives strategies.

'And No Birds Sing' is a story based on the female experience. Using the technique of third person narration and telling the story from a female point of view, it concentrates on the conflict in the protagonist's life—conflict both internal and external. The story begins thus:

> I am aware that some very young girls can hook a big fish with a simple line, but I was never one of these. My bait was all wrong, I suppose. I was quiet and nondescript.... And I had a horror of angling up someone else's creek.
>
> Later, much later, I reformed with a vengeance... Perhaps I was bored with my lonely bed.... suddenly I was what I had never been in all 33 years; available.

The beginning is sufficiently indicative of the central theme. It is the story of a lonely woman who has not been successful in attracting any men because of her simple looks and maybe because of her fear of 'angling up someone else's creek'. But then, it also mentions that she has become 'available'—which makes the reader expect her to do something unconventional.

The nameless protagonist of 'And No Birds Sing' is a secretary in a private office owned by Anil a handsome, successful man of 50, but a 'young 50' to quote her. Anil is married to Rupam and has two children. She feels flattered when she finds Anil paying her special attention, but once when Anil holds her hand instead of a file she reacts like a 'good girl'. Anil tries to convince her that he is very lonely and his wife is a sick person. Though she feels sorry for the man she types out her resignation and submits it to Anil 'after office hours' (43). He tears it up and pulls her against him. 'I didn't know karate so I just stayed put with my head on his tie', the helpless heroine explains defensively (43). Even otherwise, what else could be expected from a granddaughter of Patti who looked on men as 'the lords of creation' and woman 'as their willing slaves'. She recalls how her mother was advised by Patti on her wedding eve that just as in certain moods the scorpion enjoys stinging people with the pent-up venom in its tail, 'so men in their godly arrogance desired to sting their women—and a good wife always suffered her husband to do so' (44). The young bride had found the notion repellent and had tried to assert herself in the male world with the result that she became 'independent in thought and obedient in conduct', a fact which made her life wretched.

Right at this point appears a new character in the story. She is Vasanti, a total stranger to the heroine. Vasanti meets her at a party. She knows Vasanti to be the wife of an outstandingly handsome, sucessful man, Gopalan, who too meets her for the first time at that party. During the same party she has a taste of Gopalan's fondness for women. Bending her head with a coy blush and sipping Indian whisky 'for courage' she responds to his advances. How could she ever behave otherwise? 'I was much too feminine ever to disagree with him,' she says justifying herself (45).

Vasanti tells her about her husband's beastly megalomaniac ways. Thereafter whenever Vasanti happens to meet her the same recital continues. She wonders why Vasanti does this. She is the one who looks on 'husband' as 'a deputy of divinity awarded to her by her parents'. Then why does she speak ill of him? Perhaps it is because 'all decisive action was prohibited by the mere fact of being born a woman. The inferiority of her relative position was religiously accepted. But being Vasanti, she refused to suffer in silence' (46).

Vasanti tries to commit suicide and is saved by the doctors. While this incident does not have any apparent bearing on the life of the protagonist, it proves to be the turning point in her life. Vasanti's tricks and manipulations tell her the truth about her own self. With this incident in Vasanti's life the protagonist comes to confront the reality of her life. The oblivious state gets over and she starts questioning, 'Was I my sister's keeper? Was it my fault that Rupam could not—had not—fully engaged her husband's affections? Was it my fault that men of wit and charm were as rare as the phoenix' (47)? Finally she resigns from her job, takes up another, and moves into a new, and better flat in which 'absence itself has become an unshakable presence...' (49). With Anil's arrival her life had blossomed. It was full of bird song. But now no birds sing.

Vasanti's strategy to handle her straying husband without transgressing the feminine culture of the 'pativrata stri' makes the protagonist see how her own feminine strategies of acting helpless and coy can get her a man who does not belong to her. Her bait is all wrong. She knew it right from the beginning. She had a horror of 'angling up someone else's creek'. Being a daughter of a mother who 'burnt like a candle on the altar of [her] family', she cannot be a house-breaker (44).

There is 'a thematic carry-over in women's texts' says

Elizabeth Abel. So far as woman to woman relationships are concerned, in Abel's view these are always 'determined by the psychodynamics of female bonding' (Abel 1981:34). The protagonist of the story had always looked upon herself as the opposite of her pativrata mother and grandmother and yet when it came to taking a crucial decision she found that the female bonding was too deep to ignore.

The debate over 'women's language' has been an exciting area in recent studies. This is the term used by Robin Lakoff in his pioneering study called *Language and Women's Place* (1973) for the first time. He defines 'WL' (Woman's Language) as 'gender-socialised weaker style' (Lakoff 1973:45), while O'Bars has looked upon it as 'powerless speech, characteristic of different powerless groups and situations of powerlessness' (O'Bars 1980:108). Based on these earlier arguments Showalter traces 'interesting parallels between women's language and the recurring language issues in the general history of decolonisation' (Showalter 1981:192). According to all these critics, women's language is gender specific, often revealing itself in feminine strategies like space, silences, repetition of stylistic devices, image patterns and choice of words from the available culturally determined lexical range.

Both 'The Offspring' and 'And No Birds Sing' provide ample example of linguistic strategies employed by women writers. The strategy of inarticulation is used most effectively by Indira Goswami. Damayanti remains almost inarticulate. Here is a muted feminine self that does not answer back at all but at the same time does not give in either. Damayanti does exactly what she wants.

Dina Mehta's protagonist is not a muted woman. She talks. She even argues. But she does all this in a feminine way, in a woman's language of helplessness. Several examples of her language of helplessness have already been quoted and more could be cited. The strange thing about her is that she is not unaware of the marginalised status of woman in society. Her awareness flows in expressions like, 'All decisive action was prohibited to her by the mere fact of being born a woman' (46), or 'like a candle she continued to burn on the altar of our family' (44). But this never inspires her to stand for the sufferers. Like Damayanti, she is capable of action: she resigns her job, moves out of her old flat and begins a new life. But all this is done without talking to Anil.

Can women adopt traditionally male-dominated modes of writing for the articulation of female opression and desire? Mary Jacobus poses this question in her book *Women Writing and Writing About Women* (1979). She concludes her discussion with the conviction that women must stop reinscribing male words. But in the absence of 'new stories' and the 'power of naming', to recall Gilbert and Gubar, what choices do women writers have if they do not want to 'starve in silence' except to employ gender-specific strategies?

With the aid of feminine strategies these women writers present a world from a different perspective, a world in which what is said is not so important as how it is said and, what remains unsaid. To understand and appreciate these women story tellers better one has to learn to read meaning in spaces of silence. These are the 'lonely voices', to borrow Frank O'Connor's expression, which can be heard better with an awareness of female strategies—thematic, narrative as well as linguistic.

Works Cited

Abel, Elizabeth E. 1981. 'Merging Identities: The Dynamics of Female Friendship in Contemporary Fiction by Women.' *Signs*. 6. Spring.

Allen, Walter. 1981. *The Short Story in English*. Oxford: Oxford University Press.

Chodorow, Nancy. 1978. *The Reproduction of Mothering: Psychoanalysis and Sociology of Gender*. Berkeley: Berkeley University Press.

Gilbert, Sandra and Susan Gubar. 1979. *The Mad Woman in the Attic*. New Haven: Yale University Press.

Goswami, Indira. 1992. 'The Offspring.' Suresh Kohli (ed). *Savvy: Stories by Indian Women Writers*. Delhi: Arnold Publishers. 11–24.

Heilbrun, Carolyn. 1988. *Writing a Woman's Life*. New York. Ballantine Books.

Jacobus, Mary. 1979. *Women Writing and Writing About Women*. New York: Barnes & Nobel.

Kakar, Sudhir. 1978. *The Inner World: A Psychoanalytic Study of Childhood and Society in India*. Delhi: Oxford University Press.

Lakoff, Robin. 1973. 'Language and Women's Place.' In *Language and Society*. 2.

Mehta, Dina. 1992. 'And No Birds Sing.' Suresh Kohli (ed). *Savvy: Stories by Indian Women in English*. Delhi: Arnold Publishers. 43–50.

O'Bars. 1980. 'Women's Language or Powerless Language?' In *Women and Language in Literature & Society*. Ed. S. MacConnoll-Ginet et. al. New York: Praeger.

Showalter, Elaine. 1981. 'Feminist Criticism in the Wilderness.' In *Critical Inquiry*. 8.2. Winter. 179–205.

Spacks, Patricia Meyer. 1975. *The Female Imagination*. New York: Knopf.

Cheated and Exploited: Women in Kamala Das's Short Stories

D. MURALI MANOHAR

'Exploitation' and 'cheating' affect any human being either in a positive or in a negative way in this world—depending upon whether one is an exploiter and a cheat or the exploited and the cheated. Exploitation and cheating can take place in many ways such as in sex, in economic power, in work, in friendship.

This paper concerns itself only with sexual and economic exploitation, and the cheating of women by men. Men exploit and cheat women sexually by leaving the legal wife, and daughter and having a 'kept' woman; by seducing/molesting women through creating a fantasy world; by enjoying the company of woman in order to show society that they had a woman in their lives before getting married; by telling lies with regard to age and occupation so as to make the girl believe that she can lead her life peacefully. Men exploit women economically, for instance through the son neglecting the mother who has brought him up until he secures a job, and not looking after her in her old age.

Let us see how the above aspect is dealt with in Kamala Das's short stories in the collection entitled *Padmavati, The Harlot and Other Stories* (1992). I have restricted myself to this collection although there are other stories written by Kamala Das which have been published in different anthologies and journals.

In Kamala Das's fiction the attitude of men towards women has always been the same since the late 1970's when she published a short story entitled 'The Sea Lounge' (1976). In the

1980's 'That Woman' and 'The Princess of Avanti' (1988) which appear in *Padmavati* have the same theme and later stories continue to deal with the theme of women being exploited and cheated.

For centuries, a man having two women, one being the legal wife and the other, a kept woman or concubine, was more or less accepted. This is evident in the short story entitled 'That Woman'. In this story the man (who, interestingly, remains unnamed) has deserted his legal wife and a daughter, and has been living with the 'kept' woman. The daughter narrates the story with the opening lines: 'Three years ago, he had left us to live with a young woman' (Das 1992:12). When the man left three years ago he had done an injustice to his wife and daughter. Nor had he legally divorced his wife. Both wife and daughter have been affected emotionally due to the man's going away with another woman. They are, moreover affected socially—what now is their position in society? Either the man or his wife could have asked for a divorce, but neither does. By his actions, the man has exploited the weakness of his wife and daughter.

But equally, he exploits and cheats the 'kept' woman; he does not marry her and so denies her social and emotional security.

The problem intensifies when the man dies. The daughter comes to know about the death of her father from the local barber. Having heard this she intends to find out whether her father had written any will or testament or left any legacy for the other woman.

Hearing of the man's death, the wife and daughter reach the other woman's house. The daughter observes: 'I found the woman seated on the floor, her face buried in father's bosom' (14). The daughter asks the woman to leave the dead body immediately, because in 'half an hour's time, our relatives will reach here. It will be unseemly for you to be seen here' (14). Clearly, she does not want her relatives to know that her father had been involved with another woman. Ironically, the house happens to be the other woman's *own* house. Tragically, she has no place else to go. 'Where can I go?' she asks (15).

Kamala Das does not give any clues as to what made the man live with the other woman. Nor does she elucidate why the man created problems for both his legal wife and the other woman by his actions which inevitably must hurt both women.

For the other woman, there is also the problem with regard to the man's property. According to the law, the property goes to the legal wife when the husband dies. Therefore, the other woman cannot make any claims on the dead man's property. Thus she is being exploited and cheated economically by the dead man.

Inspite of this the other woman has not lost respect and concern for the dead man. The daughter observes: 'She kissed my father's feet twice' before she left the place (15). So perhaps it is not property, as the daughter thinks, that the woman was interested in; she was only interested in the dead man and her relationship with him. But this relationship, being illegal, only results in her being exploited and cheated, and further, insulted by the wife and daughter.

Another of Kamala Das's stories is about an old woman. 'The Princess of Avanti' is the story of an old woman—she is the Princess—and three men—the King of Vangarajya, the King of Kerala, and the King of Kalinga. Their age is not known. All we know is that the men are 'young' whereas the woman is old. The old woman is unmarried. For an unmarried woman the word 'wedding' is a happy word and also a sad one. Happy because, at last, she is going to celebrate her wedding; sad because it is too late to celebrate her wedding in her old age.

However, when the young men say to the old woman 'today is your wedding day', she is surprised (16). She says: 'Is it true?... Is it at last my wedding day?' (16). In fact it is not her wedding day. But their main idea is to seduce/molest her. They exploit her unmarried status. Then the King of Kalinga says: 'We want you to select one of us as your husband' (17). The old woman seems not to have heard the words about selecting 'one of them as her husband'. Besides, the king of Vangarajya on behalf of the three, asks the old woman not to go home but remain in the park behind the bush until the gates are closed. After the park is closed, the three of them would come climbing over the wall and celebrate the wedding quietly inside the 'beautiful park'. Listening to their words the woman is overjoyed. Kamala Das writes:

> The old woman clapped her hands. She threw her hair forward and then from behind its grey strands she peeped out at the young men.

She has been transported into a fantasy world. How could she believe that she could celebrate her wedding in her old age?

Anyhow, the old woman agrees and hides in the park till the gates are closed. They come at night. When they come the old woman curiously asks: 'What do you want from me?' (18). The answer she gets from the King of Kalinga is contrary to the earlier statement. He says: 'O beautiful one, we are your husbands...' (18). She struggles to free herself from their grip, but is subjected to gang-rape. Thus, the men exploit and cheat an old woman by creating a fantasy world around her.

This story strikes me as exposing the animal behaviour of the three men, who are not to be called human beings. Is an old woman not a grandmother figure for them? Do they have no human values? Kamala Das seems to show that lust is the most dangerous passion in the world. She seems to suggest that lust has to be controlled, so that human values may be restored, preserved and safe-guarded eternally.

Another question: Why does Kamala Das give her characters these historical names? Is she trying to show that the position of women today is no better than what it was in the past?

In a short story entitled 'The Sea Lounge' we encounter yet another situation: here the woman has no option but to marry the man whom she had no intention of marrying.

In this story, a man, ironically named Satyavrata, exploits and cheats a woman after having enjoyed her company. Before that he was grateful for the love she gave him, the kindness in her letters and in her conversations with him whenever she came to the city for a holiday. After having enjoyed her company he callously refuses to marry her.

The woman does not protest but says:

> ...that's all right, I understand, please don't have a guilty conscience about me... I will marry my old beau,... that one who has been crazy about me for years. Let us not worry about it now.

The woman's casual reference to the old beau is troubling. It seems she too is cheating and exploiting but it is undeniable that she is exploited by Satyavrata.

'The Tattered Blanket' is about a mother, eighty-five years old, who has been deserted along with her widowed daughter named Kamalam, by her son Gopi. Gopi is married to Vimala, a Collector's daughter, and is employed in Delhi. He does not take his mother and sister to Delhi but leaves them to manage their lives on their own. He was provided a good education by his mother so as to secure a job in Delhi. Is it not his moral responsibility to look after his mother in her old age? Is he reluctant to look after his mother because he has married a Collector's daughter? Or is he reluctant to look after his mother because he has to look after his widowed sister also?

He visits Trivandrum, five years later. By the time he visits, the mother has become senile and cannot recognise him.

> 'Amma, this is me, your son Gopi,' he said gently. 'Gopi, what does this mean,' asked the mother. 'Is the boy's school closed?' 'Mother is like this these days,' said the sister.

Gopi's mother's words reveal that he is still a child for her.

However Gopi has a materialistic reason for the visit. He says to Kamalam:

> 'My expenses have increased,' the man said. 'Now I have four children and I can't make both ends meet. I have to maintain my status and live decently. I want to sell my share of property and carry the money back to Delhi to put it in the fixed deposit.'

As against this, the mother expects from her son only 'a new blanket to keep her warm.' Gopi had given her a blanket,

> ...years ago when he came home for vacation from his college hostel in Madras. She waits for the day when he will return to the village near Trivandrum and bring a new blanket to keep her warm. But when he does come, he comes empty-handed, though he earns two thousand five hundred rupees every month in government service... (Elias 1985:310).

One can see the writer's intention in naming the story 'The

Tattered Blanket.' This is the condition of old mothers neglected by their sons.

The fifth woman is a prostitute named Mira in the short story entitled 'A Doll for the Child Prostitute.' Mira has a frequent visitor named Krishna, a nineteen year old boy, who comes to Ayee's brothel. But Krishna tells Mira that he is twenty-four years old and has a job at a mill. Balarama Gupta writes (1993:43):

> Mira... fails to realise that she being a prostitute cannot indulge in the luxury of love and marriage.... Ignorant of the way of the world as they are, they elope, but it proves to be just a short idyll. Mira is forced to return to the brothel. For girls like Mira conjugal felicity could only be a phantom and never a reality.

By lying about his age and job Krishna has exploited and cheated Mia. Mira comes to know the facts about Krishna when Ayee asks him:

> 'How old are you, son?'... 'I am nineteen', said the boy.... Mira winced at the words.... He told me that he was twenty-four and that he had found a job at a mill. A liar. A stinking liar. (Das 1992:99–100)

One the other hand, there is the case of a girl named Rukmani, in the same short story. Rukmani, a child prostitute, wins an Inspector's affection and his fatherly concern: he even presents a doll to Rukmani. One can notice a lot of change in the Inspector when Ayee asks:

> 'Would you like to spend some time with Mira?' asked Ayee to Inspector... 'No, Lachmi Bai, I do not feel like playing with a woman today,' said the man, applying lime on the leaves of the betel carefully. 'Something has died in me today.'

The 'something' could be his visiting a brothel house, not as a duty but, to seek women in it. Kamala Das seems to suggest that even prostitutes, can change men as Rukmani changes the Inspector. However, in spite of such rare instances, the fact is that different kinds of women, of different age groups, both educated and uneducated, have been exploited and cheated. This seems to be Das's message.

Works Cited

Das, Kamala. 1992. *Padmavati, The Harlot and Other Stories*. New Delhi: Sterling.

Elias, Mohamed. 1985. 'The Short Stories of Kamala Das.' *World Literature Written in English*. 25.2 Autumn. 307–12.

Gupta, Balarama G.S. 1993. 'Indian English Women Short Story Writers: An Overview.' *Journal of English Studies*. 1. 37–49.

En-Gendering Narratives: A Reading of 'Black Horse Square'

REKHA PAPPU

The emphasis of my essay will be on *reading* practices which deploy strategies that can be identified as feminist in terms of their concerns. My reading of a short story by Ambai suggests one such reading method without necessarily claiming that it is the only permissible kind of feminist reading. The feminist framework in fact, in its refusal to be prescriptive, incorporates a plurality of methods which enables critiques of male-centred texts and reading practices. The problem in such a context would be to identify the reading practice that would best serve feminist interests without at the same time replicating the hierarchies of the earlier discourses. I will therefore also use Ambai's short story as a pretext for discussing theoretical issues regarding language use, reading practices and feminism.

For my understanding of 'language', I rely on Julia Kristeva's conceptualisation which defines language as a discursive practice thereby shifting the emphasis from analysis of language in terms of syntax and semantics to a consideration of the context of its use as well. Kristeva argues that linguists have for too long treated language as a monolithic *system* and have restricted their analysis of language to sentence structures without problematising the basic concept of 'language' itself. She proposes instead a radical rethinking of language as a heterogenous *process* of signification.

This calls for a shift of focus away from langue, which is the system of understanding shared by a particular linguistic community, to an analysis of the speaking subject—a speaking subject who is not the transcendental Cartesian ego but is instead recognised as overdetermined and fragmented following from the Marxist and Freudian modes of interpretation.

A definition of language that is not merely restricted to the structure of sentences would allow a study of the language of a narrative for elements such as 'its ideological, political and psychoanalytic articulations, its relations with society with psyche and not least with other texts' (Toril Moi 1985:155). Therefore, it is this kind of a comprehensive understanding of language that informs my approach to Ambai's work. My reading of Ambai's story 'Black Horse Square' is based on a translation of the work. The question of translatability of languages and the relation of the language of the original composition (Tamil) to the language of the translated (English) would lead to an analysis different from that I have provided here. However, my reading does not focus on the issue of translation but instead engages with the concerns that the text itself articulates about language use.

I have divided my paper into two sections: the first deals with the debates within feminist theory regarding language use by women writers and modes of approach to texts that bear their signature. The second section following from the first will analyse 'Black Horse Square',[1] a short story by Ambai (Holmstrom 1992).

I

A question that has continually exercised feminists is the manner in which women's writing should be read so that it aligns itself with *feminist* interests. The debates in this area seem to be without closure—at times suggesting perhaps an absence of change and resolution of some kind. Therefore, it has to be emphasised that due to feminist interventions, transformation at the political and material level *has* taken place. However, these debates continue to rage, because feminist gains have at various points been reappropriated by different interest groups so that at times they subserve the very interests that they seek to subvert. Or, there is the realisation that certain feminist practices themselves are not egalitarian. Also, different alliances that feminists make necessitate rethinking. Consequently, they impel rearticulation of the feminist discourse and feminist interests.

I will begin by recapitulating the debates around feminist reading practices. This overview of the discussion derives largely from the western context and from a reading of feminist literary critics like Elaine Showalter, Annette Kolodony, Sandra Gilbert and Susan Gubar, Judith Fetterley, Judith Newton, Deborah Rosenfelt, Ann Rosalind Jones, Michele Barrett, Mary Jacobus, Helene Cixous, Julia Kristeva and in the Indian context, Susie Tharu.[2]

Feminists in the Anglo-American academies of the fifties and the sixties were preoccupied with the question of whether women's writing was essentially different from male writing and if so how this difference was marked or indicated. An extension of this problematic was whether the difference was mainly in terms of the themes considered by women writers or whether there was a language use and language structure specific to women writers which would then mark their texts as feminist. Simone de Beauvoir's assertion that women write differently not because they have wombs but because they learn to become women, emphasises the cultural and materialist aspect of gender construction. It also foregrounds the view that the experience of being a woman necessarily writes itself into the texts that they produce. Many feminist readings therefore emphasised the representation of women's experiences as also the resistance implicit in women's texts to male dominance and oppression.

However, as Judith Newton and Deborah Rosenfelt point out in their introduction to *Feminist Criticism and Social Change* (1985), in reading representations of women's experiences in women's texts, there is the danger of constructing these experiences in terms that are universal and unchangeable. Such a reading derives from the assumption that there is a reality outside the text that has to be captured by the writer. Also, such a theory does not account for the fact that women themselves may have internalised the power relationships and may end up representing them. Moreover, in invoking experience as the criterion for difference there is always the danger of being trapped within the binary oppositions of male and female. Such a viewpoint risks an insistence on the kind of biologistic essentialism that feminism has been contesting.

A risk of this kind is more marked in the case of the French feminists who argue for *'l'ecriture feminine'*. The French feminists, like Helene Cixous and Luce Irigaray, argue that for women to 'write their bodies' would be a gesture of emancipation because language systems as they exist in patriarchy do not allow women scope to articulate their experiences. Western philosophy has, according to them, systematically erased/silenced women's experience of pleasure in their bodies and therefore to speak of this pleasure or *joussiance* would be a first step towards reclaiming discourse. In this context of understanding, their theorising strains towards the creation of a new language for women. This project, though admirable in its energy and intention, is fraught with problems, the major one being of universalising experiences of women.

In the context of post-Structuralist and Derridean thought, the concept of a single author who is the progenitor of meaning is radically questioned and the stress is on the free play of textuality. Can one then still argue for a differential as well as a preferential reading of writing by women, the signature of the woman writer making a difference to the reading? How does one construct a way of reading texts so that these limitations are overcome and feminist interests served at the same time?

I find Sneja Gunew's article, 'Authenticity and the Writing Cure: Reading Some Migrant Women's Writings' (1988) very useful as a way out of this seeming impasse. Gunew uses Catherine Belsey's notion of the subject-in-process and Althusser's conception of interpellation to read some migrant women's writing in the Australian context. Belsey's notion of the subject is one that is created in discourse since discourse is also the site of meaning.[3] The importance of this notion of subject-in-progress is that it challenges the idea of a unified and well-formed subject while correspondingly emphasising the possibility of transformation. Gunew also uses Althusser's notion of interpellation to argue that '[m]igrant writing carries within it… the dead or repressed or fading subjects created by other and sometimes former interpellations' (118). Different interpellations may lead to a fragmented subjectivity and Gunew argues that a reading of this fragmentation could be one of the reading strategies for feminists to adopt. The usefulness of Gunew's approach is that it does not hinge entirely on the identity of the author/writer but on the different interpellations that the text records. A feminist reading practice could therefore analyse the different ways in which a woman is interpellated as also the resultant recognition/misrecognition.

II

I want to read in 'Black Horse Square' some concerns that seem marginal to the narrative—concerns however that repeatedly turn up as unresolved questions especially at moments of crisis in the narrative. I want to analyse what it is about these issues that compel addressal and why these particular issues become important to a narrative that locates the response of a woman who has been raped and of other women who seek to help her as central to it. My analysis of 'Black Horse Square', will at times echo some of the paradoxes that I have been discussing in the last section pointing perhaps to the difficulty of the task of feminist reading which is, to borrow Kolodony's phrase, something like 'dancing through the minefield'.

'Black Horse Square' identifies itself in the text as a 'report'. The opening line of the story reads: 'This is a report to one who lives by reason rather than emotion' (Holmstrom: 109). There are other references as well to the story being a report as when the narrator repeats and elaborates on her intention: 'I am trying to write this precisely, without unnecessary emotion, knowing you to be a Marxist who claims to be calm and logical at all times, considering each matter as carefully as it were on a pair of scales. Whether I shall be successful, I don't know' (112).

Different nuances are built around the term 'report'. The narrative structure of 'Black Horse Square' belies expectations about what a report should be through formalistic devices such as pluralty of perspective and circularity of narrative. Yet it insists on calling itself a report. The expectations of language use and structure within a report is what the narrative brings into question and the gesture of naming itself as a report is revealed as obviously parodic. The account that the narrator gives her husband and which she calls a report (the rules of reportage demanding that it should be rational in its exposition and devoid of emotion), is counterposed within the narrative itself against the reports of newspapers and magazines. The narrator points out that in the early news reports about Rosa's rape case, 'there is a certain lack of concern' (119). Rosa herself is scornful about reports and her contempt is evident when she refuses help from members of an organisation but instead tells them: 'Go and write up your reports: Rosa has been raped, she must have justice' (121).

The only kind of report that the narrative gives legitimacy to is one that manages to communicate feelings and emotions. In the concluding part of 'Black Horse Square', for example, the narrator says: 'This report is a mere bundle of words. If somewhere among these words you can find a life-thread, grasp hold of it. It must be there somewhere, surely, breathing life. Let it be the first syllable of a new language' (135).

Corresponding with the concern about the ambiguous nature of reports, the question of language also becomes important. The narrator repeatedly refers to the failure of language to communicate feelings and emotions at different points in the narrative. 'As we learnt more and more words, somewhere we lost all real connections' (117). A similar sense of despair about incommunicability is expressed in the statement: 'How is it possible to translate that gesture into words?' (128).

These observations when counterposed against comments that valorise language of a different nature suggest an attempt at changing the understanding of language.

> People like your mother have their own special language. It seems to possess the kind of structure, the heights and depths of the language of words. Yet it is wordless. It is a language embedded in the swinging of arms, in the glance of the eye, in the pressing of a hand against the back, in laughter, in weeping, in lamentation, in the silence that does away with all words. And it is this other language that separates us and them. Even if we speak to each other in a language which we mutually understand, we only comunicate facts. Our language is a mere bridge. It strikes me that we are seeking a different language; one that does not enforce divisions, but links and bonds together. The language one understands as soon as a child lifts her outspread hands (130).

Even at the beginning of the narrative, Abhilasha writes to Lenin:

'To understand that which has not been captured in this writing, you will have to come here. You should look into her dry, tearless eyes. You must make that silence that comes from her your own. And burn in it' (109).

These comments suggest that a distinction should be made between the language expressed by the speaking and gesturing subject on the one hand and the general understanding of the meaning of linguistic units shared by a linguistic community on the other. Language in itself is not meaningful. The context and manner of its articulation shape the understanding. Also, as Kristeva suggests, when the subjectivity of the speaker is taken into consideration, the articulations would probably yield meanings that might not correspond directly with the meaning of the linguistic units.

In 'Black Horse Square', Rosa emphasises this difference in subjectivity when she says: 'Between you and me there is a huge difference. And I'm not referring to the difference between your sari and mine. There is a more profound difference. Nobody has raped you and torn you apart. As I have been. I have been torn; my blood has been spilt. This joins us. But it separates us too' (120). The narrative thereby rejects a simplistic equation of all women's experience but instead codes comprehension as deriving from an understanding of the discourses which create subjectivities and their specific modes of articulation. By shifting emphasis to the speaking subject, the narrative focusses on modes of understanding that should necessarily be differential because subject positions are constructed differentially.

I have focussed on the narrative's preoccupation with the notion of reporting and the question of language because they are to a large extent configured by the confrontation that the narrative stages between emotion and reason. The subjectivity of the woman narrator of 'Black Horse Square' is constructed as emotional in contrast with her rational husband. She attributes his rational nature to his identity as a communist and not specifically (as one would expect) to his masculinity. However, the accusation of rationality (it has to be termed as such because the narrative builds up emotional responses as positive and reason as unfeeling, uncaring and cold-blooded, all of which form the negative pole which is marked as necessarily the opposite of emotionality) in the narrative later shifts to the identity of the intellectuals. When Rosa's husband, Prabhakar Shinde, in a heated discussion with Lenin (the narrator's husband) asks him, 'Can you intellectuals shed a tear over this? Do you have tears to shed, any of you?' (124), it would suggest that Prabhakar Shinde, a man, is also against the kind of system that does not admit of feelings.

The shifting locations of emotionalism suggest (until this point) that it (emotionalism) is neither a female trait nor an exclusive male preserve. The markers in the narrative which repeatedly target reason, however, make it clear that emotion itself is privileged over reason. The narrative's seemingly consistent effort to not assign certain structures of behaviour and response either to women or to men is placed under severe constraints because in hegemonic discourses men and women are differently interpellated. This difference leads to a slippage in the narrative itself and these interpellations get registered accordingly.

The first reporter who makes a caustic remark about the demonstration by women against rape is not marked as male or female. The remark attributed to the reporter reads: 'It is clear that the Association against Rape are not a branch of any particular political party. They have a very wide appeal, it is true. It seems they haven't even left Jesus Christ alone.' The reporter who next appears in the narrative *is* gendered and is gendered as male. The comment made by this reporter reads: 'I have one doubt. Watching some of the women in the procession, it was difficult to tell whether they were men or women. Is this the independence that women seek? Are these the proper clothes to wear to a demonstration protesting against rape?' (133). The narrative comment appended to this is: 'So wrote this Tamil journalist, out to protect Tamil culture and revealing his Tamil manliness' (133).

My reading might suggest precisely the point that I have been contesting in the earlier section regarding the 'reality' outside necessarily making its way into the text. To mark my difference I reiterate that my emphasis is on what Gunew calls the 'ideological loadings of interpellation' (118) which are registered not as complete and coherent but which might lead to misrecognition and fragmentation. The marks of contest that the text reveals between different interpellatory modes undermines the notion of a monolithic reality and composite subjects while emphasising the notion of changing discourses and subjects-in-process.

The contradictory signals encoded in 'Black Horse Square' are pointers to its negotiation with the interpellations that are recorded. The narrator, for instance, would be interpellated as a woman as well as an educated individual. Education and intellection is associated in most discourses (and in the narrative itself) with reason. As pointed out earlier, in 'Black Horse Square', emotion is privileged over reason. The need for a defense of emotionality becomes clear when one recognises that hegemonic discourses figure the woman as emotional and irrational and so place women's responses at the negative axis of the value system. A remark by Gopal Sharma, a TV studio employee is telling in this context. When approached to cover the demonstration, he replies, 'Oh yes, we'll cover it. But it will have to be without sound. We'll do the commentary. Who knows what you women are likely to say' (Holmstrom: 135).

The ideal language (which is linked to the degree of emotion that it manages to communicate) that the narrator refers to each time is that of a woman—of Rosa, Rosa's mother and an old woman called Kasibai. Therefore, the contradiction that I read in 'Black Horse Square' is its refusal, on the one hand, to assign certain values exclusively to either women or men (and to thus undermine the negative import of those values) and its compulsion on the other hand to defend emotionality and so by extension, women themselves. The narrative seems to initially resist designating and categorising values between masculinity and femininity. The compulsion to valorise emotion however leads to the narrative shifting values, that it codes as positive, to women.

This compulsion to privilege emotion itself, I would argue, follows from the interpellatory modes that hail women as emotional and men as rational and therefore women as inferior and men as superior. In a move that seeks to reverse this value system, the narrative assigns a positive value to emotionality and hence to women and a negative value to rationality and so to men. However, the politics of and the function of these interpellations themselves are unquestioned. Emotionality is still a largely female preserve and rationality a male one. An implication of such a formulation could be that women should vacate the domain of reason which even if for different reasons aligns this viewpoint with the predominantly male argument that women are incapable of reasoning.

I have tried to show through my analysis of 'Black Horse Square' that a strategy of reading that considers the manner in which the text negotiates the contradictory interpellations of different discourses might benefit feminists. It not only emphasises the process by which subjectivity is formed but also reveals the historical reasons that makes women 'an unstable category' (Riley 1988:3) thereby opening up the possibility of changing/challenging it.

Notes

1. Anthologised in *A Purple Sea* (1992) edited and translated by Lakshmi Holmstrom. The method of reading that I provide here of the short story is one that can be used, with some variations, for other narrative forms as well. I use 'Black Horse Square' because of its preoccupation with language use, an aspect that I focus on here.
2. Since this section provides an overview of the context within which I wish to propose a feminist reading practice, I have provided a brief summary of the arguments that were put forth within the history of academic feminism. I have not provided detailed discussion of any one critic or reading practice in spite of the rich and textured nature of their works.
3. I use the term 'discourse' in the sense that Emile Beneveniste and Louis Althusser discuss it:

   > Beneveniste describes discourse as a signifying transaction between two persons, one of whom addresses the other, and in the process defines himself or herself. The French Marxist philosopher Louis Althusser helps us to understand that discourse may also consist of an exchange between a person and a cultural agent, i.e. a person or a textual construct which relays ideological information (Silverman 1983:48).

Works Cited

Gunew, Sneja. 1968. 'Authenticity and the Writing Cure: Reading Some Migrant Women's Writing.' Susan Sheridan (ed.). *Grafts: Feminist Cultural Criticism*. London: Verso. 111–23.

Holmstrom, Lakshmi (ed). 1992. *A Purple Sea*. New Delhi: Affiliated East-West Press Limited.

Moi, Toril. 1985. *Sexual/Textual Politics: Feminist Literary Theory*. London: Methuen.

Newton, Judith and Deborah Rosenfelt. 1985. *Feminist Criticism and Social Change*. London: Methuen.

Riley, Denise. 1988. *Am I That Name?: Feminism and the Category of 'Women' in History*. London. Macmillan.

Silverman, Kaja. 1983. *The Subject of Semiotics*. New York: Oxford University Press.

Student Responses to an Intermediate Text: A Case Study

NIRMALA RITA NAIR

The First Year Intermediate non-detailed[1] text book in Andhra Pradesh is an anthology of nine short stories.[2] Three of these have been written by Indians and the remaining are by American and European writers. The Preface of this anthology states that it has been chosen by the Board of Intermediate Examination with the intention of providing 'good exercise in reading and entertainment to the student at the Intermediate stage'. However, has this been achieved? To answer this it is necessary to find out what the student encounters in the text.

The title of the first short story is 'The Love-Philtre of Ikey Schoenstein.' As the student is still wondering what 'Love-Philtre' means, how Ikey is to be pronounced, will it be possible to remember the spelling of Schoenstein correctly, s/he is confronted with the following introductory passages:

> The Blue Light Drug Store is... between the Bowery and First Avenue...
>
> It macerates its opium and percolates its own laudanum and paregoric. The store is on a corner about which coveys of ragged-plumed, hilarious children play and become candidates for the cough drops and soothing syrups that wait for them inside.
>
> Ikey Schoenstein was the night clerk of the Blue Light.... Ikey's corniform, be-spectacled nose and narrow, knowledge-bowed figure was well known in the vicinity of the Blue Light...

> ...The circumlocution has been in vain—you must have guessed it—Ikey adored Rosy. She tinctured all his thoughts; she was the compound extract of all that was chemically pure and officinal—the dispensatory contained nothing equal to her. But Ikey was timid, and his hopes remained insoluble in the menstruum of his backwardness and fears.

Will a student find the above lines readable and enjoyable?

This paper attempts to explore and analyse the reponses of Intermediate students to 'The Love-Philtre of Ikey Schoenstein' and other such stories. It seeks to ascertain whether the language in these stories is a source of help or is a hindrance in reading and understanding them.

This paper reports the findings of a survey conducted in St. Francis Junior College for Women and St. Mary's Centenary Junior College, both of Secunderabad. Students were interviewed individually and in groups to elicit their responses to the short stories in general and to the Indian short stories in particular.

While analysing the students' attitudes to and understanding of the Indian short story as compared with those written by American and European writers, it was observed that the language of the stories by the latter was 'complicated and difficult'. Although the youngsters enjoyed reading stories by Maupassant and Maugham, since this helped them to widen their horizons, the fact remains that to many students the language in these particular stories was difficult to decipher. O. Henry's story 'The Love-Philtre' is a case in point.

Ikey loves Rosy. To prevent losing her, Ikey plays foul. When he is asked by Chunk McGowan for a powder that excites love, Ikey gives him morphia instead. He then informs Rosy's father about Chunk's plans for eloping with Rosy. However, Ikey unwittingly facilitates rather than foils the couple's plans to escape. For, the sleeping potion that was meant for Rosy is consumed by Mr. Riddle, enabling Rosy and Chunk to hurry away and get married. Thus Ikey's plan boomerangs on him.

Students liked this story and the surprising turn that events take, but they definitely did not like its language. In this paper 'The Love-Philtre' has been taken as an example of a story by a western writer where the language becomes an obstacle to understanding.

Of the Indian short stories prescribed for study, attention has been mainly focussed on 'The Castaway' by Rabindranath Tagore since it is an ideal example of a short story that the average Indian student can read with ease. The factors that make this possible are first listed and then discussed at length. They are:

1. Simplicity of language and style.
2. Familiarity with location and culture.

I

'The Castaway' by Tagore is a story about Nilakanta, a young Brahmin boy, who is a member of a theatrical company. When his boat founders in a storm, he swims ashore at Sharat's garden steps and is allowed to stay on in the house. The introductory passages in 'The Castaway' clearly convey many important details about the atmosphere, the place, the main characters and the topic of their conversation. There is a description of the Ganges 'lashed into fury' (7) followed by the picture of a quiet 'closed room of one of the riverside houses at Chandranagore' (7) in which a young couple are engaged in a discussion:

> The husband, Sharat, was young: 'I wish you would stay a few more days; you would then be able to return home quite strong again.'
>
> The wife, Kiran, was saying, 'I have quite recovered already. It will not, cannot possibly, do me any harm to go home now.'

Kiran is bored with her lonely and monotonous life at Chandranagore since 'there was nothing to do, there were no interesting neighbours, and she hated to be busy all day with medicine and diet' (8).

Nilakanta's appearance therefore, adds a new dimension to her life and she involves herself in caring for his well-being. 'She made a dandy of him with Sharat's cast off clothes and also gave him new ones' (9). Besides food and clothes, she bestows on him her affection and attention. She is curious to learn more about him and often calls him to her room to recite pieces from his repertoire. 'Thus the long afternoon hours passed merrily away'.

However, when Sharat's brother Satish comes to spend his college vacation with them, Kiran is delighted and spends time in 'games and quarrels and reconciliations and laughter and even tears' (12). Poor Nilakanta is forgotten. 'He felt that he would like to be a knife to cut Satish to pieces; a needle to pierce him through and through; a fire to burn him to ashes. But Satish was not even scared. It was only his own heart that bled and bled' (15). Filled with bitterness, Nilakanta thrashes his innocent boy-followers and kicks his pet mongrel. He cannot openly reveal his enemity to Satish. 'But he would contrive a hundred petty ways of causing him annoyance' (14). On one occasion Nilakanta over-reaches himself when he conceals Satish's favourite ink-stand only to irritate him. Satish and Sharat are convinced that Nilakanta has stolen it. Only Kiran refuses to believe it. But when circumstantial evidence makes Nilakanta appear to be a thief in the eyes of Kiran, he is unable to bear the pain and so he leaves the place and goes away. It is the simplicity of language and style that enabled students to respond intellectually and emotionally to this story.

Tagore's language offers a sharp contrast to the language used by O. Henry in 'The Love-Philtre'. Besides pharmaceutical terms and words of rare usage, there is a generous sprinkling of unfamiliar phrases, epithets and idioms. For instance:

> We've been *laying pipes* for the getaway...
>
> ...I'm afraid *she'll stand me up* when it *comes to the scratch*...
>
> ...she'll never regret *'flyin' the coop* with Chunk McGowan.
>
> It's all dead easy if Rosy *don't balk when the flag drops* (emphases mine).

Students were baffled by the words and phrases italicised above. It is also important to note that many of these unfamiliar words have been used only once in the text. Consequently, they remain unfamiliar.

Does this imply that students are averse to new and difficult words? Not necessarily. The fact is that students would like to learn new words depending upon the manner in which these words are used. For instance in the story 'The Interview' by Khushwant Singh, the word *numismatics* (i.e. a study of coins and medals) is the hub around which the story revolves. This humorous tale is about a Public Relations Officer who pretends to know the meaning of this word and as a consequence finds himself in an unenviable predicament. Students enjoyed reading this story. Long after studying it they could not only recall the word *numismatics* but also its meaning.

Students found it difficult to cope with the literary style of western writers chosen for study since their vocabulary was unfamiliar and their sentences were lengthy and complex. O. Henry's description of Ikey is an apt example:

> Behind his counter he was a superior being, calmly conscious of special knowledge and worth; outside he was a weak-kneed purblind motorman cursed rambler, with ill-fitting clothes stained with chemicals and smelling of socotrine of aloes and valerinate of ammonia....

Compare this with the vivid description of a character by Mulk Raj Anand who uses a few simple words to paint a pen picture of Munshi Singh in 'A Promoter of Quarrels':

> 'Ayaji', a pale young Sikh boy answered, with his head bent and his chin thrust back in abject humility.... Munshi came, showing his ribs and knees through his torn long tunic and pyjamas....

Yet the very mention of the short story 'A Promotor of Quarrels' was met with groans and grimaces. Students felt that this story was not easy to read. Discussions revealed the following blocks to reading and understanding the story:

1. The use of coarse and vulgar language to depict the quarrel between Basanto and Hiro, two poor cowherd women.
2. The insults and curses, when translated into English seem to sound extra awkward and unpleasant.
   Their ugliness seems to be magnified. For example:

   > I will comb your matted hair with a firebrand, you bitch! You daughter of a pimp and a whore! I will pour the boiling water of my rage on your head! I will eat you alive!

3. There were mixed reactions regarding the idioms that were translated literally. The idiom 'There is something black in the pulse' was greeted cheerfully with many students calling out the Hindi equivalent. However, the literal translation of unfamiliar proverbs and idioms made it difficult to understand them as is evident in the examples given below:

   (i) …we have to pay the grazing tax to the Sarkar before we can leave, or they will take our clothes off.

   (ii) Go like the dog! Come like the cat! Go, go eater of your masters.

Few students enjoyed reading the story. In fact, many plainly stated that they disliked it. In the words of a student: 'There is nothing wrong with the story. It is the correct picture of the life of certain kinds of people, but it is not correct for the Intermediate Board to make us study it.'

This paper does not brand all western stories as incomprehensible and hail all Indian stories as easy, enjoyable and understandable or vice versa. The focus is on the stories chosen for study in the Intermediate text book of which 'The Love-Philtre' appears to be difficult while 'The Castaway' seems to be lucid and clear.

The concluding paragraphs of the 'The Castaway' and 'The Love-Philtre' are a study in contrast for they highlight the different literary styles adopted by O. Henry and Tagore respectively. The paragraph for perusal is from O. Henry's 'The Love-Philtre':

> 'Oh, that stuff you gave me!' said Chunk, broadening his grin; 'well, it was this way. I sat down at the supper table last night at Riddle's, and I looked at Rosy, and I says to myself! Chunk if you get the girl get her on the square—don't try any hocus-pocus with a thoroughbred like her. And I keeps the paper you give me in my pocket. And then my lamps fall on another party present, who, I says to myself, is failin' a proper affection toward his comin' son-in-law, so I watches my chance and dumps that powder in old man Riddle's coffee—see?'

Compare the above paragraph with Tagore's concluding lines in 'The Castaway':

> The whole family went home. In a day the garden became desolate. And only that starving mongrel of Nilakanta's remained prowling along the river banks whining and whining as if its heart would break.

The passage from 'The Love-Philtre' is important from the point of view of the story. However the use of complex sentences, unfamiliar phrases and idioms and the use of a dialect makes it difficult to read and understand. The passage from 'The Castaway', on the other hand, is not only simple and easy but also touching.

II

Other factors which make the Indian short story easily understood include familiarity with the setting, the customs and the culture.

For instance, it was difficult to visualise 'snowdrifts' and 'trees silvered with hoar-frost' in 'Vanka' (19). However it was easy to picture the vivid opening scene in 'The Castaway' with its terrific downpour of rain, 'crash of thunder... repeated lashes of lightning...' and trees swaying 'from side to side sighing and groaning' (7). Similarly, it was enjoyable to read about the pranks of Nilakanta and his young friends and their escapades as a result of which 'not a single mango tree in the neighbourhood had the chance of ripening that season' (9). It was easy to understand the manner in which Kiran teases Satish by suddenly clasping his eyes from behind. The young readers knew why Nilakanta refused to eat when his feelings were hurt since some of them had done the same thing themselves. The adolescents understood this gesture of refusing to eat as a means of registering anger or sorrow, or attracting attention or sympathy.

Besides the use of complicated language, the depiction of strange places made it difficult to visualise persons and conditions and achieve a proper understanding of a story. For some students the names of characters of different nationalities were difficult to remember and/or spell. A few of the names that were considered problematic have been listed below:

1. Ivan Vanka Jukov, Constantin Makatrich, Viune and Kashtanka, Pelagea, Aliakhine, Olga Ignatievna, Fedia, Egor and Aliona (in 'Vanka' by Chekhov).
2. Paolo Saverini, Antoine, Semillante, Nicolas Ravolati (in 'Vendetta' by Maupassant).

Students could identify with characters whose names were similar to their own. Perhaps for this reason the names of the characters in the short story 'The Castaway'—Satish, Sharat, Kiran and Nilakanta—were remembered long after they were read and studied.

Similarly, it was difficult to imagine far-away places with strange sounding names such as the following: Bonifacio, Ajjacio, Sardinia, Longosardo (in 'Vendetta' by Maupassant).

The names of places mentioned by Tagore in 'The Castaway' were Chandranagore and Calcutta. Need it be stated that these names were easily remembered?

Students find it easier to read stories that depict a society concerned with values and problems that they can understand. For instance, although many students disliked 'A Promoter of Quarrels', they were familiar with the world that it portrayed—they had seen unscrupulous merchants like Nanak Chand who were caste-conscious, who cheated their customers and who oppressed their poor workers. They had also witnessed poverty-stricken women quarrelling among themselves instead of uniting to fight for justice.

On the other hand, although the story 'Vanka' appealed to students there were occasions when it eluded understanding as evidenced in the following examples:

Viune knew how to steal a moujik's chicken….

The mistress took a herring and thrust its 'phiz' into Vanka's face.

III

From this survey it became evident that students welcomed the opportunity to read stories by western writers since it widened their horizons. However, proper undersanding of these stories was impaired for the following reasons:

1. It was not easy to read certain passages since they included pharmaceutical terms, as in O. Henry, as well as words that were difficult or rarely used
2. Sentences were sometimes long and rambling, making it difficult to decipher them
3. Some sentences were confusing since they contained more than one idea
4. Ideas were not conveyed in a simple and clear manner but were shrouded in irony, sarcasm and subtlety.

Similar problems also exist in the text prescribed for detailed study. However, these obstacles to reading and understanding take on added significance in the case of the non-detailed text. For, this text is not only meant to make students interested in the English language but it also aims at making them interested in extra reading, reading rapidly and inculcating self-study habits.

Intermediate Course: Stories From Far And Near, the non-detailed text being examined with its use of different dialects, difficult vocabulary and structures does little to arouse in students an interest in the English language. It sometimes has the opposite effect. Students who find the language difficult prefer to study from guides. This happens despite the efforts of teachers to make the lessons intelligible and interesting. The difficulty arises perhaps because of the problems involved in teaching large numbers of students (sometimes a hundred or more) in each class, besides lecturing for as many as three, four or even five hours a day, conducting tests regularly and correcting literally hundreds of papers. The English lecturer, unlike the teachers of optional subjects, teaches students who are doing the Sciences, Commerce and Social Sciences, and therefore cannot possibly remember and cater to the different academic needs of all these students in different classes. Despite these problems, teachers in both the colleges (where this survey was conducted) have made attempts in the past to help the disadvantaged students by offering them remedial courses.[3]

Another method of enabling students to read the text with ease would be to prepare a simplified version of the text as has been done with the Second Year Intermediate non-detailed text.

While an intensive remedial course and a simplified version of the text may be helpful, what is really needed is the preparation of a new non-detailed text which is related to the text prescribed for detailed study. Such a non-detailed text which consolidates the vocabulary which the student has acquired and gradually introduces new vocabulary will be relevant and useful.

There is another, simpler way in which the Board of Intermediate Examination can succeed in inspiring and encouraging students to read English: viz. by prescribing a book by an Indian writer. There is another reason why such a book would be preferable. Students are put to inconvenience since the Intermediate text books are often in short supply. However, if the book is by an Indian author the scenario would be different. For instance, if R.K. Narayan's *Swami and Friends* is prescribed for study, students will be able to procure a copy of it without any difficulty.

Many students felt that it would be a welcome change if the text to be studied was a novel or short story collection by Tagore, Premchand, Anita Desai or Khushwant Singh. Interestingly almost all the students were of the opinion that they would enjoy studying *Swami and Friends* or *Malgudi Days* by R.K. Narayan.[4]

This choice re-affirms the point that for a short story to be understood and enjoyed by students, it should be written in simple and easy prose, it should have an interesting story, it should be set among people and places one is familiar with and it should *not* be difficult to understand. A passage like the following by Somerset Maugham in 'A Friend in Need' is difficult:

> Why novels and plays are so often untrue to life is because their authors, perhaps of necessity, make their characters all of a piece. They cannot afford to make them self-contradictory, for then they become incomprehensible, and yet self-contradictory is what most of us are. We are a haphazard bundle of inconsistent qualities. In books on logic they will tell you that it is absurd to say that yellow is tubular or gratitude heavier than air; but in that mixture of incongruities that makes up the self, yellow may very well be a horse and cart and gratitude the middle of next week. I shrug my shoulders when people tell me that their

> first impressions of a person are always right... For my own part I find that the longer I know people the more they puzzle me... (31).

These lines about the mysterious aspect of human nature remained 'incomprehensible' and a 'puzzle' to most students. Stories that are replete with difficult and obscure words may lead students to dislike literature and develop a repugnance for reading. Hence, a great deal of care and effort need to be invested by the Board of Intermediate Education to ensure that the stories chosen for study do indeed provide 'good exercise in reading and entertainment to the students at the Intermediate stage'.

Notes

1. The Intermediate class is a stage between school and college and is equivalent to classes 11 and 12. Not all States in India have an Intermediate class. Non-detailed texts are additional texts studied in class with the intention of encouraging rapid reading, and comprehension.
2. All page numbers in the paper are with reference to *Intermediate Course: Stories From Far and Near*, First Year Non-Detailed Text, Board of Intermediate Education, Andhra Pradesh, 1992.
3. Sr. Doris Cooper, Principal, St. Francis Junior College for Women, Secunderabad, observes that on the academic front Intermediate students come from different media and backgrounds but are expected to follow the same English text books. These students face difficulties in learning English. Sr. Cooper is of the opinion that the social, cultural, economic and psychological disadvantages of such students necessitate special assistance in the form of an intensive remedial course.
4. How would students respond in such a step? This is best answered in the words of a student: 'We like stories by Indians because they write about people who live like us, living in our kind of world; we are familiar with the things they are talking about.'

The Indian Short Story: Towards a Location Chart

S. VISWANATHAN

'English and the Indian Short Story.' One should think that the conjunction 'and' in the title has meanings and suggestions beyond the merely linear, juxtapositional denotation of the connective. It looks as though the Indian short story, no matter whether written in English or in an Indian language, may ultimately be seen to have to do with 'English' in some sense or other.

The relationship the Indian literary genre of the short story, as we generally understand it, bears to its English counterpart, applying the epithet 'English' in the extended sense of 'western,' is manifold. The relationship has to be considered in terms of not only the question of the influence of English models of the genre but also of the impact of English and western values, mores and manners on the depiction of life in the Indian short story, something parallel to but not identical with the impact of western values and attitudes, habits and customs, and, we might add, gestures and nuances, on life and life-style in general. The influence, it is true, can present itself as the 'anxiety of influence' and 'resistance' as, for example, in the early stories of Raja Rao or the pieces of short fiction of K. Nagarajan, to mention instances within Indo-English fiction. Indeed, the argument may be advanced that hegemonisation by English is so pervasive in general and so insidiously imbedded in the short story in India that a programmatic liberating campaign has long since been due, a campaign at least in our deployment of critical perspectives and standards. In some of these perspectives the operativeness of 'English' in its linguistic and literary identities may be traced (to use prepositional terminology), in, on, around, over, above, behind and beneath the Indian short story. To vary the prepositional into the conjunctional, it is at the least 'English and the Indian Short Story'. More provocatively, it is 'English *vs.* the Indian Short Story'. In many an example there is an English overlay or underlay, subtext or context or implicit rival text, assimilated or contended with. Contestatory or non-contestatory as the nativisation of the genre may be, it would be seen to trace such forms as these—the deliberate use by some short story writers of dialects of our regional languages, the specialisation in the inflections and minutiae of our native cultural being and living, a focus on rural themes, rural life and rural idiom, the harking back to the pattern and motifs of purana and legend and ancient lore, and most important, the cultivation of modes, techniques and tonalities of the older, often oral traditions of 'katha' and 'upanyasa' discourses, or of folk narrative. These are perhaps the directions in which the modern western phenomenon of the short story has been sought to be indigenised into something like the 'upakatha' of our tradition.

While these contrapuntal patterns of relationship of the genre to 'English' in a broad sense have to be taken into account, the fact remains that English is a presence in the Indian short story. The Indian short story is perhaps best viewed as a distinct, divergent development in the country of the western form that originally arose in the nineteenth century in America, France and England. There is a school of opinion which would rather regard the Indian short story as tracing its line of descent back to native Indian traditions of short fiction and fictional and fabulatory narration. One need not deny the certainly active factors of native influence on the short story in India. Among these are the orality of the old tradition, the important native techniques of fiction and the fabular orientation as well as the symbolist dimensions of our narrative tradition. These latter could potentially offer viable alternatives to the realism and naturalism of western or English fiction. The tradition of the fabulatory or, to use another term, the tradition of the apologue, is so much part of the age-old habits of story-telling of India. The Upanishadic stories often cast in the form of dialogues and discussions, and the inset stories and episodes of the *Mahabharata* are among the earliest examples. A western approximation to the apologue-like fiction is to be found in such works as Johnson's *Rasselas*, partly Goldsmith's *The Vicar of Wakefield* and a novel of the early nineteenth century with Indian setting and theme like Lady Morgan's (Sydney Owenson) *The Missionary*, in which novels, thus called, there is an overplus of discussion of ideas, morals and philosophy. It is in a way understandable that *Rasselas* and *The Vicar of Wakefield* were very widely read and appreciated in late nineteenth-century and early twentieth-century India. The Indian modes of apologue-like fiction could be seen to have re-emerged in certain varieties of parabolic fiction. Some examples of these kinds of novels and short stories which contain a dominant element of meditative discourse and discussion of ideas are Raja Rao's stories and novels, a number of stories with a conscious or unconscious parabolic orientation which appear in our Indian language magazines and collections, and certain early examples of short fiction such as B.R. Rajam Iyer's *Vasudeva Sastri* and Subrahmanya Bharathi's short stories, especially those featuring his favourite character of Milagaipazhasamiyar. By the same argument, the short stories of Hardy which constitute an interesting set of examples of the sensitive portrayal of change in rural life and values amidst the clash of tradition and modernity were almost totally neglected by readers in our country in sharp contrast to the immense popularity of Hardy's novels here, and this resulted in a relevant model which could have served as a point of departure being ignored. Alongside these factors we may have to consider the possibilities of the influence of the fictional techniques of the stories in our ancient collections (like *Kathasaritsagara*, Gunadya's *Brihatkatha* and the Buddhist *Jakata* tales) on modern fiction as a whole including the European evolution of fiction. Such influence could have originated not only from the *Panchatantra* and *Hitopadesa* modes of fabulation but also from devices like the frame story, the story-within-the-story, the dream or vision framework, the picaresque motif, the handling of the past and the future in story and other narrative concepts and means exemplified in the old Indian story collections like *Brihatkatha* and *Kathasaritsagara*.

All the same, while we give due weight to all these native currents of influence on the short story in India, there is perhaps not much warrant for views of the Indian development of the form as bearing mainly an adversarial relationship to Eurocentric models. The history of the advent and evolution of the short story in India cannot at any rate be dissociated from the influence of English in the short story available to the early Indian practitioners of the genre. These were the stories of Kipling, H.G. Wells, Bennett, Maugham, H.E. Bates, 'Saki' and more prominently, of Poe and O. Henry on the one side and Chekhov and Maupassant on the other. It is interesting that Kipling, a pioneer of the short story, published his earlier stories in India. These models were the ones that mediated the form into the country; the French and Russian short stories were generally accessible in English translation. Perhaps a select minority of short story writers in our languages could and did go directly to French or Russian models. No wonder that the relationship of our Indo-English novelists to short story writers bears certain resemblances to the relationships between English novelists and short-story writers. Both the groups would seem to have used the two mediums to very similar purposes and effects.

The Indo-English fictionists however, would seem to have practised the short story genre much less extensively and on a smaller scale than long fiction. One reason for their 'shortness' on the short story, was the lack of a large enough forum in the English newspapers and magazines in the country. It is, after all, the phenomenal growth of the forums in England and the west in the very late nineteenth and early twentieth centuries that led to the emergence of the short story as a strong literary form. By the same argument, the growth of Indian language newspapers and magazines, helped the quick and rich growth of the short story in our regional literatures.

When it comes to the use of English in Indo-English fiction, one may venture the surmise that the language is handled with better ease and naturalness and with a certain inwardness in the Indo-English short stories of the same fictionists than in their regular novels. Such an argument is perhaps applicable to certain western English writers, for instance, to Somerset Maugham, a sort of a stylist, whose style works to better effect and greater fictional advantage in his short stories. In Indo-English, short story writers at their best have succeeded not merely in a certain indigenisation of the genre and an indigenisation of the English language but have interiorised the language and the genre. The use of Indian modes of understanding and Indian idioms and turns of expressional phrasing in English, all this is part or ought to be part, of this process of interiorisation. As we say, they could think and feel in and through the language instead of merely using it as a means of communication.

In this respect, it is interesting that the new generation of old Stephenians and civil-service and business world writers, in their fictional engagement, resulting in an all but phenomenal output, have left the short story practically untouched, while they have generally shown, as it has often been remarked, a confidence and inwardness with English as a medium of thought, sensibility and expression. It may not be out of place to remember in this connection T.S. Eliot's statement in one of his essays to the effect that the acquisition of a second language is tantamount to the acquisition of a second personality. That is, it is adding a new dimensionality and enrichment to one's personal make-up. It is not, certainly, splitting one's personality.

This linguistic-cultural consideration may be applied in a different way to writers in Indian languages who insert English into their short stories. English figures in their short stories sometimes as a way of characterising or 'placing' or exposing particular characters who snobbishly or for other reasons affect English, sometimes as borrowed English words and expressions which have acclimatised themselves in the usage of Indian languages. This is as it should be. One may be thankful that the purist tendency which promotes the invention and coinage of linguistic equivalents to terms like 'bus', 'train', and 'hotel', did not affect our short story writers. After all, the English words and expressions find their way into the speeches of the short story characters and in the narrative writing of the authorial personae in a manner similar to that in which they occur in day-to-day Indian speech. These interspersings of English make for an interesting heteroglossia and thus add to the polyphonic possibilities in the Indian language short story.

Before concluding, it is worth noting a few other features of the role of English in Indian story writing. A considerable number of Indian stories in English published in the early part of the century, not exactly short stories but often serving for the genre in anthologies and collections, were renderings in the form or an approximation to it, of old Indian legends or historical incidents and events of the past. Sister Nivedita, Tagore's now forgotten sister, Swarnakumari Goshal who published two volumes of stories, an English teacher like Michael Madhusudan Dutt are examples of this kind. And these through the medium of English did help the promotion of an awareness of our history and tradition in their young readers. F.W. Bain is another similar but also different example, for he made up stories in English in imitation of old Indian stories and parables.

As all of us have increasingly come to realise, the availability of the rich short story literature in our regional languages from one to the other language and to the world at large is to be facilitated by translation into English. This enterprise has to flourish as it bids fair to do at the moment, alongside the enterprise of other inter-linguistic translations of short story and other literatures within the Indian linguistic map.

English, thus, in its varying and varied roles will continue to be with the Indian short story.

Contributors

P.A. ABRAHAM teaches English at Sana'a University, Yemen. He has published several articles and book reviews in leading journals and newspapers. He has also published *Sherwood Anderson and the American Short Story*. He visited the University of Toronto and the University of Western Ontario on a Fellowship awarded by the Shastri Indo-Canadian Institute. He was a Salzburg Fellow and Secretary, Indian Association for Canadian Studies.

ASHOKAMITRAN (also known as J. Thyagarajan) is a well-known writer in Tamil. He has been publishing extensively since 1954. He is a novelist and short story writer, critic and translator. His works have been translated into almost all major Indian and foreign languages. Currently, two novels, *The Eighteenth Parallel* and *Water*, and two collections of short stories, *The Colours of Evil* and *A Most Truthful Picture* are available in English translation.

LAKSHMI CHANDRA works in the Department of Distance Education at CIEFL, Hyderabad. She has had varied research and teaching experience and has edited and published material for Distance Education departments. Her areas of interest include the teaching of English and American Literature. She has published *Fiction as History: The Works of Katherine Anne Porter* and co-authored *Improve Your Writing* and *Learn English for Science*.

RANJANA HARISH teaches in Gujarat University, Ahmedabad. She has several research papers to her credit and has published *Indian Women's Autobiographies, The Female Footprints, Achhot* and

Niji Aakash. She is an established writer in Gujarati and Hindi. She was an Indo-Canadian Shastri Fellow in Canada and a visiting scholar at UCLA. She is an Associate of the Indian Institute of Advanced Studies, Shimla.

M. KESHAV is an education administrator in Kendriya Vidyalaya Sanghatan. He has an M.A. from Sri Krishnadevaraya University, Anantapur, and an M. Phil from the University of Hyderabad. His interests are Commonwealth Literature and Telugu Literature.

SUDHAKAR MARATHE teaches in the Department of English, University of Hyderabad and is interested in fiction, eighteenth-century literature, Eliot and Shakespeare, criticism and translation. He has published several critical articles in scholarly journals both in English and Marathi. He has to his credit several poems and translations. He has published *T.S. Eliot's Shakespeare Criticism, Read First, Criticise Afterwards: Reading and its Pedagogic Value* and *Cocoon* an English translation of Nemade's Marathi novel *Kosla*. He was a recipient of the Katha award for translation in 1992.

SACHIDANANDA MOHANTY teaches English at the University of Hyderabad. He has authored two books on D.H. Lawrence, edited three others including *In Search of Wonder*, a book on cultural exchange for the India Fulbright Commission, and his essays and translations have appeared in some of the leading journals in the country. He won the Katha award for outstanding translation in 1992 and the Katha-British Council Translation Prize in 1994. He was a British Council Scholar, a Fulbright Fellow at the University of Texas at Austin and Yale and a Salzburg Fellow. He held a UGC Career Award and researched women's writing in Orissa.

TUTUN MUKHERJEE teaches English at the Osmania University and has specialised in Literary Criticism and Critical Theory. Her publications include books and articles on criticism, American Literature, Women's Studies, Translation and Film Studies. She is a recipient of the UGC Career Award for research in Bengali folktales.

D. MURALI MANOHAR teaches English in the University of

Hyderabad. He has an M.A. and M.Phil. from the Department of English, University of Hyderabad. His research work is on the man-woman relationship in Kamala Das's poetry. His areas of interest are Indian writing in English and Women's Studies.

NIRMALA RITA NAIR is based in Hyderabad. She did her Ph.D. on the fiction of Eudora Welty. She is interested in American literature, particularly women's literature of the South, and aspects of the Indo-British literary and cultural encounter.

REKHA PAPPU is the Coordinator of Anveshi Research Centre for Women's Studies, Hyderabad. She has worked on reconceptualising Nation, Community and Gender for her Ph.D. Her research interests include Gender and Legal Studies.

K. SANTHANAM is a teacher of English at the Jamal Mohamed College, Tiruchirapalli. He has contributed articles to several scholarly journals. His interests include American, British, Canadian, African, Indo-Anglian, and Comparative Literatures, Contemporary Literary Criticism, Journalism and Mass Media. He is a recipient of a Faculty Research Award from the Shastri Indo-Canadian Institute.

VASANTHI SANKARANARAYANAN is a film scholar based in Chennai and has a Ph.D. on Malayalam Cinema. She has translated from Malayalam into English and has done projects for leading publishers in India.

M. SRIDHAR works in the Department of English, University of Hyderabad. He did his Ph.D. on F.R. Leavis. His interests include literary criticism and translation. He has published *The Woman Unbound: Selected Short Stories*, a joint translation of the Telugu writer Volga. Another collection of translations from Telugu is in press.

T. SRIRAMAN works in the Department of Distance Education, CIEFL, Hyderabad. His Ph.D. dissertation was a study of Lionel Trilling in relation to the Arnoldian tradition in criticism. He has published coursebooks in English language and literature. His interests include grammar and usage and stylistics.

ALLADI UMA teaches in the Department of English, University of Hyderabad. Her interests include African-American Literature,

Women's Studies, translation and Indian writing in English. She has published *The Woman Unbound: Selected Short Stories*, a joint translation of the Telugu writer Volga. Another collection of translations from Telugu is in press. She was a Fulbright Scholar at Yale University.

S. VISWANATHAN is a retired Professor of English. His interests include Elizabethan, Seventeenth-century and Victorian literatures and Twentieth-century literary criticism. He has contributed numerous articles to reputed national and international journals. His books are *The Shakespeare Play as Poem: A Critical Tradition in Perspective* and *On Shakespeare's Theatre Language*. He was a Commonwealth Staff Fellow at Kent University, Canterbury and Visiting Fellow at Queen's University of Belfast. He was also a UGC Emeritus Fellow.

The Editors

MOHAN RAMANAN teaches in the Department of English, University of Hyderabad. He has published over a hundred articles in India and abroad on modern poetry, American literature and Indian Writing in English. He is the author of two books and the editor of several others. He was British Council Scholar at Merton College, Oxford, and Fulbright Scholar in Residence at Amherst College, Massachusetts. He was Senior Academic Fellow at the American Studies Research Centre, Hyderabad.

PINGALI SAILAJA teaches in the Department of English, University of Hyderabad. She is a linguist with interests in Generative Morphology and Phonology, Language acquisition, Stylistics and English Language Teaching. She has co-edited several books, and is the author of *Issues in Lexical Phonology*.